The Collected Supernatural and Weird Fiction of James Hain Friswell

—Ghost Stories and Phantom Fancies—

The Collected Supernatural and Weird Fiction of James Hain Friswell

—Ghost Stories and Phantom Fancies—

One Novelette 'The King of the Gnomes,'
Ten Short Stories and One Poem
of the Strange and Unusual

James Hain Friswell

LEONAUR

The Collected
Supernatural and Weird
Fiction of
James Hain Friswell
—Ghost Stories and Phantom Fancies—
One Novelette 'The King of the Gnomes,'
Ten Short Stories and One Poem of the Strange and Unusual
by James Hain Friswell

First published under the title
Ghost Stories and Phantom Fancies

Leonaur is an imprint of Oakpast Ltd

Copyright in this form © 2012 Oakpast Ltd

ISBN: 978-0-85706-902-3 (hardcover)
ISBN: 978-0-85706-903-0 (softcover)

http://www.leonaur.com

Publisher's Notes

The views expressed in this book are not necessarily
those of the publisher.

Contents

To

THE GENTLEWOMEN OF MY FAMILY,

AT HOME AND ABROAD,

THIS LITTLE BOOK:

IS DEDICATED

WITH

RESPECT, KIND WISHES, AND LOVE

Prefaces

An Interlocutory Preface

Scene 1.—A Railway Carriage.

Two young ladies in compartments on the same side; Author in one *ditto* opposite them.

Caroline. Have you read Mr. Jogglebury's new book?

Edith. Yes, dear; very stupid, is it not?"

Caroline. Quite so; but oh, there's such a dear, delightful, dreadful ghost legend! I sat up late one night reading it; and oh-o-o-o! [*She here describes the usual sensations when the candle went out at the proper moment.*]

Edith. I dearly love ghost stories.

Caroline. So do I.

Author (*mentally*). So do I, when you get them good. I will call to aid a friend or two, and give the public the benefit.

Public. And here, we suppose, is the book. (*Which surmise is quite correct.*)

Preface

Scene 2.—*Author appears as a popular lecturer.*

Spirits are at a discount. I do not mean those spirits the total annihilation of which my friend George Cruikshank would rejoice at, but I refer to those gentle, tricksy, pathetic spirits; those gaunt, grim, and dreadful spirits; those awfully ghastly and ghostly spirits, who awoke our sympathies and made us cry, or who rattled chains and half frightened us to death, some years ago. No one believes in them now. Mrs. Radclyffe, to be sure, made an attempt to revive some faint resemblance to the original old ghost, but anyone could see that the lady's creations were half sham, and generally resolved themselves into dim shadows, waxen images, dreams, or pictures, in a manner so as to make you doubt, when awakened from your enchantment, whether the reader, the writer, or the heroine of the story—who was involved in such a turmoil of nothing, such a storm in a teacup—was the greater fool.

Horace Walpole, of Strawberry-hill, Esquire, had put his foot into the business long before, and with about the same result as that which would accompany the same action performed by a donkey on a basket of eggs. In his story of *The Castle of Otranto*, he makes a ghost's nose bleed, and I really think that that small mistake of the author finished, so to speak, the romantic existence of ghosts forever. Henceforward future Coleridges may conclude *Christabel* with the very genius of the first author; future La Motte Fouqués write other *Undines*; and later Tassos again create *Rinaldos* in the enchanted wood; but the reign of the veritable ghost is over. If, which is highly improbable, we have another Shakespeare, we may perhaps hope for a second Hamlet; but most assuredly the ghost will be left out.

The modern age, which believes in impossible percentages, honest directors, political economy, financial reform, spirit-rapping, a virtuous aristocracy, and other such miracles, hath exploded ghosts; and yet, of all the figments of the brain that you and I wot of, I really do not know anything more thoroughly respectable and unquestionable than your ghost. He always appeared for a purpose; that purpose was always good; and he always accomplished that purpose. He was a *Deus ex machinâ* appealed to upon particular occasions to set these odds all even.

Was there a rich tyrant, the author of I don't know how many murders, seated easily on his throne, utterly careless of the curses of priests, the sighs of virgins, the prayers of parents, and the tears of orphans, your ghost appeared, shook the wretch to his centre—his inmost core they call it at the transpontine theatres—and sent him howling to——a monastery. Was there a poor man whose grandfather, being possessed of wealth, had sunk his capital in a bank (of a hedge, not the British), straight the ghost appears, will not let the poor man rest until he, wandering forth in the moonlight, sees the figure pointing with downward finger to the spot where the immense treasure is invested.

Ghosts are always doing kind offices, and yet they have been invariably shunned. They are ever found to be the right persons in the right place, and yet we first dread them, and then doubt them. There is not, I believe, on record, an authentic instance of the appearance of one of these spirits—from the ghost in *Hamlet* to the wooden apparition in the drama of *Punch*—of which it can be said that it has not fulfilled its mission. There are other missionaries of whom we cannot, with due respect, say the same.

The following book is, therefore, an attempt, not to revive an exploded superstition, but to rescue a creature of the human brain from most undeserved neglect. The writer, like the prince of Denmark, exclaims, "Alas! poor Ghost!" and at this present Christmas time, and at other times too, when, drawing round the fire, we delight in stories of the superhuman and the marvellous, seeks, by a simple and a kindly fiction, to beguile the time, to exercise the imagination, and, it is hoped, to leave the heart not unimproved.

London,
December, 1857.

All Alone on Christmas Day

So it happened. I am not called upon to explain how it was, but I state the fact. I was alone, quite alone, on Christmas Day.

I am a married man and a father. I had not quarrelled with my wife, nor had I beaten my children. I, on the contrary, kissed and petted them before I went, bid my wife be of good cheer, told the girl to be especially good and the boy to surpass every boy living, and set forward on my journey to my appointed task.

I was not going to prison; I was not in a lock-up house; I was not in hiding—nor in attendance upon a sick friend; I was simply alone. A good dinner was provided for me; and I sat down, and, with a mental grace, eat it thankfully. Christmas Day had not lately been a cheerful day to me. I had had old family jars, troubles, which acting perhaps upon a mind envious of others' happiness and comfort and joys, had made me morbid upon that day, when all—I think so now—should rejoice. I had relations, too, who used to be with me in my boyhood, who used to pet and welcome me upon that day, who were now far enough away. One, with as stout a heart as ever beat, was working, with a little colonial brood around him, in another hemisphere, and upon a hot Christmas Day would be recalling the snow and icicles, the merry slides, the junketings and feastings, of an English Christmas. Two others, brave girls grown into English women, had formed other ties, were almost aliens, and lived where Christmas was not Christmas at all, being under the old *régime*, and having been kept off for twelve days yet.

They would recollect; would they ever forget it? Do English hearts ever forget the old home ties, the childhood's games, the least remembrance of the rough old land which gave them birth? They forget! Pish! Tut! They thought of me and I of them, although I was all alone.

I turned round my chair and pushed away my decanter of wine, and sat gazing at the fire. The ghosts of many a past Christmas rose tip before me. Now of that when I was a little boy, playing at a child's game of "Bow to the wittiest, kneel to the prettiest, and kiss the one you love best,"—and when I had knelt to my own little sister and kissed my mother; how the people all laughed, and my mother blushed, half with shame and half with pleasure, and told me that I should be more polite. More polite! why more polite? Society had not falsified me then. Did I not think my little sister the prettiest lady in the world, and love my mother better than anyone else? The first was, I thought then—and I think so now—prettier than the grand beauty of the room, about whom all the men crowded, and for whose sake half of them wished to be children, and to play in the midst of that circle, amongst which she, with a charming *coquetry*, danced and played.

I did not like that grand beauty, with her *beaux yeux*, her curls so artfully arranged, her fine white shoulders, and her scented hair. Nor did I like, half so well as my little five-year sister, the other beauty, who was a little *passée*, to be sure, but who had plenty of jewels about her, having made a very good match, and who was so anxious that the diamond butterfly in her black hair should tremble in the light, and the brilliant *collier* should rise and fall and give forth its thousand sparkles from her neck. I was but a little child, but *I* knew why she breathed so hard, that beautiful woman! A wit of the party said that the diamonds shone with an inspired lustre. I did not understand the words, but I divined the meaning.

That Christmas Day is long past. Others came, less merry—days of penance and weariness—days spent with a severe grandmother, who, being an invalid, would make her son and grandson live with her. She had a spite against me, I know: she used to give me the drumstick of a tough turkey for dinner. She was not of a religious turn, or she might have "improved" the occasion. No! She was a dozen times worse than that. She was a severe, worldly woman, wise as a serpent; and used systematically to set to work pulling and rooting up the flowers of romance or merriness or jollity which grew about a young heart, as a gardener would root up weeds.

I should have respected an old dame who fancied it was wicked to go to a play; but I could only despise an old creature whose chief objection to the theatre lay in the money which was required before the check-taker permitted you to pass. Those Christmas Days are gone—gone with the good feasts, the laughter, the sighs, the dances, the old sirloins of beef, and aristocratic puddings which graced them,—gone with the crackled and dried holly and the withered mistletoe—withered as if laid in the sarcophagus of a mummy,—gone forever, and my penance had gone with them! So be it!

Then came other Christmas Days. I was a boy—a man. I had man's cares, and was much thought of. I had come into my man's estate—I was one of the great world. Let no one—no, not if he hath not inherited so much as one penny-piece—despise that heritage. It may not promise much; but it is golden—golden and full of promise, if but used rightly. How was it that upon my first Christmas of my manhood, we children gathered— the party had broken up, the guests had gone, and the candles were low in the socket—we children gathered round my mother, and danced, and, joining hands as our hearts joined, danced round her in a ring, and wished her the joy of the night. There were two elder brothers there; the one a big fellow from the country—the other a sharp lawyer, with a family; both of them joined in the dance, and kicked and capped madly. How was it that, with a prophetic kindness, half laughing, half in tears, our mother covered her face, and told us that another Christmas would come when the circle would be broken.

It came, indeed—the circle was unbroken, thank God. Though

I cannot stretch my hand far enough to reach theirs, and though we may never, never in this world, form in that Christmas ring again, it was and is unbroken now,—but the centre of the radius was gone, and but a segment lives in England. I thought—of course I did, as I sat alone—upon that Christmas.

Not wholly on myself were my thoughts wasted. I thought of the hundreds whom I had met in my passage to my solitary dinner; of those who were hurrying to some friend's house, of the greetings, tidings, tears, welcome, and hand-shakings of the day. I thought of the good old people who might not see another such day, and of those who looked forwards to fifty more before they left this earth. I peopled the room with Christmas people. Christmas in the hall, Christmas in the workhouse, Christmas in the far-off midland counties—and again Christmas, out at sea.

I thanked God for the day, for its influence and the lesson which it taught; for the old friends brought together, the enemies made friends, the old ties cemented, the new ones formed. I thought of—and I am happy to say I counted two or three of—the happy homes, which out of my strange prison I could have visited and have made happy by my presence. I drank the health in the last bumper of my pint of wine of all I knew, and closing my eyes to recall the faces, felt somewhat sad to think I was alone.

Alone! why bless me no! How is this? There is a circle round the fire. One, two, three, four, absolutely six or seven people. Strangers too. No, not quite strangers. I fancy I have seen some of these gentlemen before. All men have types of faces; some of these I should know. There is the—but I will not describe them. You, will know them by the stories they relate.

My guests—visitors—what shall I call them?—are talking. Upon what subject do you think they have the impudence to talk? They positively—ghosts themselves—are speaking about ghosts. It seems as hardy to me, as if being seated in the stone kitchen, or any famous resort of thieves, the conversation should fall upon burglaries and such-like eccentricities indulged in by men of an erratic genius. One of my new friends, evidently a learned young gentleman, quotes plenty of recognized instances of the ghost real. Another, a dogmatic man in black, only admits the ghost to exist in the imagination; a third, whose faith is of that easy description, often met with in the world, which will believe in the most extraordinary miracle if you can only give it a scientific turn, weighs and balances the chances for and against, taps the ghost, so to speak, gauges his probability, puts him to spirit proof, and after a little while learnedly pronounces the world to be too matter-of-fact, too material, too reasonable to believe in anything like ghosts. Ghosts! ha! ha! he! he! the gentleman gives a thin, dry, hollow laugh which sounds much as if you were to rattle a quantity of rusks in a bag, and produce a rustling.

My state during this conversation may be imagined. Here was I, surrounded by phantoms—so to speak—things removable by a breath, certainly not tangible (by the way, I had an odd sort of dread of putting that to the proof)—hearing them bandy reasons about their own existence! And one of these figments absolutely talking about the reason, the common sense of the world—a world which he had left, if I could judge from his box-bottom trousers, stiff pudding cravat, and high-collared coat with brass buttons, about the time when Messrs. Tom and Jerry first distinguished themselves in the annals of that important but unrecognized empire, "High Life."

I could hold out no longer; I was positively bursting with indignation. "'Pon my word, gentlemen," I cried, filling myself a glass of wine—the decanter, I am bound to confess, rattling against the glass with a tremor of indignation: "'Pon my word, gentlemen—this is funny, this is humorous! *You* to doubt of ghosts! Why, you will be questioning spirit-rapping next, and asserting that the world is too sensible to believe in *that*."

I had no sooner given vent to my opinion in words, of which it, is curious to relate, I myself heard no sound, than all the phantom guests before spoken of turned round and looked at me, and then at each other. When I mentioned spirit-rapping they fell a-laughing as heartily as they could, making a noise which a great authority has likened to the "crackling of thorns under a pot."

"As for spirit-rapping, good sir—as for spirit-rapping," said the Tom-and-Jerry ghost, "we know something about that—don't we?" He turned round to the others with a dry humour, and borrowing a couple of rib-bones from a stout fellow who sat by his side, began to use them as clappers, and made such a rattling noise, which was taken up by every corner of the room with the most perfect echo, that I could not but doubt that I had discovered the true cause of this extraordinary phenomenon. He then returned the bones, and said, with a solemn face, "Why, sir, I tell you what it is: the world has believed, does believe, and will believe any nonsense you choose to tell it; it has a perverse disinclination to truth; but give it any absurdly romantic error and it will believe it right off the reel, as the Americans say. We have been a good deal in America since that spirit-rapping came up."

"But," said I, "*à propos* of ghosts, do you believe them?"

"Table-moving—do you believe *that*?" answered my interlocutor. "In fact, do you believe in a thousand queer stories, odd ideas, vain fancies, absurd relations, which somehow or other get abroad and get mixed in the common creed? Why not in ghosts? They are very good fellows; they hurt no one, tread upon no-body's toes, only amuse—sometimes warn and teach!"

"Warn and teach!" cried the rest of the company, in hollow voices. "For myself, I love a ghost. Ghosts are jolly fellows!"

"All jolly fellows!" said the rest.

The sound which came forth from their united throats was again the faintest echo of a sound, and yet it made the glasses which were on the buffet ring again. I thought of rising and going away; but directly I did so, a young clerical ghost, with an M. B. waistcoat, a muslin collar, and a tonsure, who I saw at once had been a Catholic priest, fixed me with a look. Like the ancient mariner did unto the wedding guest, so did he unto me: he held me by his eye.

"Perhaps," I faltered, "perhaps, gentlemen, you would not object, now the conversation turns that way, to spend the rest of the evening in telling me your experience in this matter. It will be one way of spending Christmas Day; unless, indeed," I added, "you have an objection to that being named." I said this because I had a dim idea that ghosts did not like Christmas.

"Not in the least," answered the priest, "not in the least; why should we? We love Christmas as we love our ties to earth. Not the gross, the sinful, and the sordid,—they are gone and die away; and, even with mortals, at this holy season are more weak than at other times. But we love those which were generous, kindly, and good; we remember the love which bore no ill to its brother; we love to dwell upon the days when peace and good-will reigned; when little ilk were forgotten and forgiven; when the head grew wise enough to overlook an error, and the heart kind enough to forgive one.

All my fears vanished in a moment what I heard the kindly tones of the "Nun's priest." (I had given him that name because I fancied some resemblance must lie between him and the gentleman who bears that name in Chaucer.) I at once proposed that the stories should begin. I settled myself cosily in my chair, and, being enamoured of the priestly ghost, held out my hand to grasp his. The result, I am bound to say, leaves me still in doubt as to the personality of ghosts. My hand came in contact with nothing more spiritual than the poker, which I took hold of, and, having poked the fire, looked as if I were ready to listen to any amount of legends.

My visitors interpreting my desire—as expressed, I am sure, in my speaking countenance—rightly, whispered among themselves, and, without further preface, commenced that which the reader may become acquainted with if he will but turn over the next page. I must let him know, however, that they continually addressed their narratives to each other; that they did not narrate, wholly, their personal experience; and that I omit, in this truthful narration, many interruptions which I had to put up with. The Tom and Jerry gentleman, who, I take it, had been a commercial traveller, evidently fancied that he was again in the flesh, and commences his story accordingly. The Anglo-French ghost, the spirit of a gentleman who, being connected with mercantile affairs, had dwelt for a long time at Lyons, at Paris, and at other French towns, relates merely that which was related to him.

Looked into closely, their narrations might just as well have been told by living, rather than spiritual, beings; but I have noticed through life that ghosts, spirits, and other mysteries which we come across, never do satisfactorily explain themselves. Like children who see fairies let down upon a stage, and who still wish to examine the ropes and machinery, not knowing that the enchantment would then vanish, we, common humanity, desire to look at the springs of unearthly action.

"Oh," cries an American writer, "Oh, if the spirits of Napoleon, Lord Byron, Shakespeare, and King Henry VIII. would only come upon earth, sit down in our editorial chair, *and be talked to*—what would we not elucidate?"—to which we answer that, although the process would be doubtlessly very interesting to the editor, it might not be so to the ghosts; and that they are of a very kingly nature, and like the apparition of Hamlet's father, being so majestical, will not suffer the least show of violence. It results, therefore, in this—that the more ghosts we see, the more spirits we hear rap, the less we know about them; and we hereby give notice that the present book only deals with them for its own purposes, and is not going to attempt to popularise any scientific information concerning them.

The Dead Man's Story

On a dreary night in December, three gentlemen were seated in a painter's studio. The night was intensely dark and cold, and a slight hail beat against the window with a monotonous and ceaseless noise.

The studio was immense and gloomy, the sole light within it proceeding from a stove, around which the three were seated. Although they were bold, and of the age when men are most jovial, the conversation had taken, in spite of their efforts to the contrary, a reflection from the dull weather without, and their jokes and, frivolity were soon exhausted.

In addition to the light which issued from the crannies in the stove, there was another emitted from a bowl of spirits, which was ceaselessly stirred by one of the young men, as he poured from an antique silver ladle some of the flaming spirit into the quaint old glasses from which the students drank. The blue flame of the spirit lighted up in a wild and fantastic manner the surrounding objects in the room, so that the heads of old prophets, of satyrs, or Madonnas, clothed in the same ghastly hue, seemed to move and to dance along the walls like a fantastic procession of the dead; and the vast room, which in the daytime sparkled with the creations of genius, seemed now, in its alternate darkness and sulphuric light, to be peopled with its dreams.

Each time also that the silver spoon agitated the liquid, strange shadows traced themselves along the walls, hideous and of fantastic form. Unearthly tints spread also upon the hangings of the studio, from the old bearded prophet of Michael Angelo to those eccentric caricatures which the artist had scrawled upon his walls, and which resembled an army of demons that one sees in a dream, or such as Goya has painted; whilst the lull and rise of the tempest without but added to the fantastic and nervous feeling which pervaded those within.

Besides this, to add to the terror which was creeping •over the three occupants of the room, each time that they looked at each other they appeared with faces of a blue tone, with eyes fixed and glittering like live embers, and with pale lips and sunken cheeks; but the most fearful object of all was that of a plaster mask taken from the face of an intimate friend but lately dead, which, hanging near the window, let the light from the spirit fall upon its face, turned three parts towards them, which gave it a strange, vivid, and mocking expression.

All people have felt the influence of large and dark rooms, such as Hoffman has portrayed and Rembrandt has painted; and all the world has experienced those wild and unaccountable terrors—panics without a cause—which seize on one like a spontaneous fever, at the sight of objects to which a stray glimpse of the moon or a feeble ray from a lamp give a mysterious form; nay, all, we should imagine, have at some period of their lives found themselves by the side of a friend, in a dark and dismal chamber, listening to some wild story, which so enchains them, that although the mere lighting of a candle could put an end to their terror, they would not do so; so much need has the human heart of emotions, whether they be true or false.

So it was upon the evening mentioned. The conversation of the three companions never took a direct line, but followed all the phases of their thoughts; sometimes it was light as the smoke which curled from their cigars, then for a moment fantastic as the flame of the burning spirit, and then again dark, lurid, and sombre as the smile which lit up the mask from their dead friend's face.

At last the conversation ceased altogether, and the respiration of the smokers was the only sound heard; and their cigars glowed in the dark, like Will-of-the-wisps brooding o'er a stagnant pool.

It was evident to them all, that the first who should break the silence, even if he spoke in jest, would cause in the hearts of the others a start and tremor, for each felt that he had almost unwittingly plunged into a ghastly reverie.

"Henry," at last said one, again dipping the spoon into the flaming spirit, "hast thou read Hoffman?"

"I should think so," said Henry.

"What think you of him?"

"Why, that he writes admirably; and, moreover, what is more admirable—in such a manner that you see at once he almost believes that which he relates. As for me, I know very well that when I read him of a dark night, I am obliged to creep to bed without shutting my book, and without daring to look behind me."

"Indeed; then you love the terrible and fantastic?"

"I do," said Henry.

"And what do *you* think of such romances?" said the questioner, addressing the third.

"I like them much," was the answer.

"Good; then I will tell you a strange story which happened to myself."

"I presumed as much," said Henry.

"An adventure in which you are the hero?" said the third.

"Yes, I myself. I must again before I commence assure you that I am the hero of this strange adventure."

"Go on, then; we will listen."

The silver spoon fell from his fingers into the bowl; the flame of the spirit, not enlivened by agitation, faded out little by little, and in a few moments they were in almost complete darkness, a warm light only being thrown upon their legs by the fire in the stove.

He began his story:—

"One mid-winter evening, it might be about a year ago, the weather was just as it is now—the same cold, the same sleet and hail, the same dullness. You know my profession is that of a surgeon, and on that day I had a great many cases to attend; so that after having made my last visit, instead of going, as sometimes I did, to the theatre, I made haste home. I then dwelt in one of the most deserted streets of the Faubourg Saint Germain. I was very tired and I quickly got to bed. I extinguished the lamp and amused myself with gazing at my fire, watching the great shadows which each little flame made dance upon my bed-curtains; then at last my eyes shut, and I fell asleep.

"It might have been an hour after I first closed my eyes, when I felt some person shaking me roughly. I woke with a start, and in not the very best temper, and stared with some surprise at my nocturnal visitor. It was my manservant.

"'Sir,' said he, 'rise at once; you are sent for to a young lady who is dying.'

"'Where does she live?' said I.

"'Nearly opposite; but there is a messenger downstairs who will take you to her.'

"I rose, and thinking that at such a moment my toilet was of little consequence, dressed myself in haste. I took my instrument-case, and followed the man who had come for me.

"It rained in torrents. Happily, however, I had only the street to cross; and I was almost immediately at the house of the person who required my assistance. She dwelt in a large and aristocratic hotel. I had to cross a wide court-yard, and to ascend a stone staircase which ran up outside the building: then, passing a vestibule, wherein some servants were waiting to show me upstairs, I was at once conducted to the chamber of the sick lady. It was a very large room, furnished throughout with oaken furniture very ancient and beautifully carved.

"A maid-servant showed me into the chamber, and then left me. I went at once to the bedside, carved like the rest of the furniture, with tall pillars running up to some height, supporting a canopy of rich arras, and upon which, pressing a snowy pillow, lay a head more ravishing than ever Raphael dreamed of when he painted his finest Madonna. Locks, bright and golden as a wave of Pactolus, floated round her face. Her eyes were nearly closed, and her mouth partly open, discovering a row of teeth beautifully even and as white as pearls. Her neck surpassed the lily in whiteness; and when I took her hand I saw so fine an arm, that it recalled to me those which Homer has assigned to Juno.

"I remained there, forgetful of the cause for which I came, gazing at her, and recalling nothing like her in my recollections or my dreams; when she turned towards me, and opening her large blue eyes, said to me, 'I suffer much.'

"Still there was, I found, little the matter with her. I took my lancet, but at the moment of touching an arm so beautiful and white, my hand trembled. However, the feelings of the doctor triumphed over those of the man; I opened a vein—there came from her blood pure and bright as melted coral—she fainted.

"I did not wish to quit her. I remained with her. I felt a secret happiness in holding, as it were, the life of so beautiful a being in my hands. I stanched the blood; she opened her eyes by degrees, carried the hand she had free to her bosom, turned towards me, and fixed upon me a grateful look. 'Thank you,' she said, 'I suffer less.'

"She had about her such beauty that I felt rooted to my place, counting each pulsation of my heart against each throb of her pulse; listening to her respiration, which each time grew less feverish, and thinking to myself that if ever there existed a heaven upon earth, it must be in the love of such a woman as I saw before me.

"She slept!

"I remained, almost kneeling by the side of her bed. A lamp of alabaster, suspended from the ceiling, threw its golden light upon all the room. The woman who had come with me had gone away to announce that her mistress was better, and had no farther need of any of the servants. I was alone; and there she lay, calm and beautiful as an angel who has fallen asleep in the midst of a prayer! As for me—I was madly in love.

"However, I felt that I could no longer remain there; I retired, therefore, without making a noise, so as not to waken her. I ordered some little things to be given her when she woke, and I left word that I would return the next day.

"When I reached my home, I could no longer sleep. I lay awake, thinking of her. I felt that the love of such a woman would be an eternal enchantment, made up of reverie and delight. With these thoughts of her, I passed away the night; and when the day came, I was still madly in love; madly—I was a maniac!

"However, after these follies of a night so agitated, came morning's reflections. I remembered that an unfathomable abyss separated me from the loved object; that she was too beautiful *not* to have long had someone who loved and would be united to her; that she would love him so tenderly, so devotedly, that she could not forget, or be faithless to him: so I set myself to hate him without knowing who he was—this man, to whom I thought, in my mad way, that Providence had given in this world such exquisite felicity that he could submit to suffer in the next an eternity of pain without a murmur.

"I waited impatiently the hour when I could again visit her—each moment seemed an age; but at last the time came, and I set forth.

"When I arrived, I was shown into a *boudoir* furnished with the most exquisite taste, and altogether with a lavish luxury, which was shown in every article of furniture. She was alone, reading; a large robe of black velvet covered her from head to foot so completely that, like one of Perugino's angels, only her face and hands could be seen. She held coquettishly, in a scarf, the arm from which I had bled her, and was holding to the fire her two pretty little feet, which did not seem formed for our earth; and there she sat, looking so pure and beautiful that I thought her an ideal of one of the angels! She held out her hand, and bade me sit down beside her.

"'So soon up, madam,' said I: 'you are surely imprudent.'

"'No,' she said, 'I am quite strong;' she smiled sweetly as she said it; 'besides, I have slept well, and am, moreover, not very ill.'

"'You said, however, that you suffered.'

"'More in mind than body,' said she, with a sigh.

"'You are sad, madam!'

"'Oh! deeply so,' she returned; 'but happily Providence is also a physician, and has found for grief a universal panacea—forgetfulness!'

"'But,' said I, 'there are some griefs which kill.'

"'True,' she said; 'but the grave and forgetfulness, are they not the same? One is the tomb of the body, the other that of the heart. There is no other difference.'

"'But you, madam, how can you suffer grief? You are too high to be touched by it; sorrow should pass beneath you like clouds pass under the feet of angels; to us come storms and lightning—to you the blue serenity of heaven.'

"'Ah!' she said, ''tis there you deceive yourself; there all your science ends; your knowledge does not reach the heart.'

"'Well,' said I, 'try at least, madam, to forget. God sometimes permits a joy to succeed grief, and a smile to follow on our tears; and 'tis also true that when the heart of one He tries is too wide to refill of itself, and when the wound is too deep to heal without succour. He sends across the path of such a one a soul which can comprehend and know it; for He knows that we suffer less in suffering together, and that a moment must come when the desolate heart must leap again with joy, and when the deadly wound must heal.'

"'And what is the prescription, doctor,' said she, 'by which you would heal such a wound?'

"'That must be according to the patient,' I returned; 'to some I should counsel faith; to others, love!'

"'You are right,' she answered; 'they are the two sisters of charity who visit the soul.'

"Then ensued a long silence, during which I fixed my eyes upon that sweet countenance, on which the light which peeped through the silken curtains cast such a charming tint; upon those beautiful tresses, which now no longer floated over her face like a veil, but which were banded on her temples, and were drawn behind her ears. The conversation had taken from the beginning a sad cast; but by this, the beautiful being before me seemed more radiant than before, diademed as she was with the triple crown of beauty, love, and grief.

"'Thus I remained gazing at her, not so mad as I was on the first evening, but the more collected by her quietude. If that moment had made her mine, I should have fallen at her feet, I should have taken her hands, I should have wept with her as a sister; and whilst I reverenced her as an angel, should have consoled her as a woman.

"But I was yet ignorant what grief it was which she should forget, or what had caused the deep wound still unhealed; and this was what I had to find out, for between the physician and patient there was not as yet sufficient confidence for her to own her sorrow, although there had been enough for her to confess the cause. Nothing, however, that I could divine gave me the clue; no one had called at the hotel to inquire for her—none appeared to trouble themselves, as lovers would, about her. Her grief, then, must lay in the past, and must be reflected alone in the present.

"'Doctor,' said she to me, suddenly awakening from her reverie, 'can I soon dance?'

"'Yes, madam,' I answered, astonished at the question.

"'Because you must know that I must give a ball which I have promised for some long time; you must come—will you not? You will have very little opinion of my illness, which, making me dream all day, does not hinder me from dancing all night. My grief, however, is one of those which must be concealed in the depth of one's heart, so that the world may learn nothing; there are tortures which must be masked with a smile, lest anyone should guess them; mine I wish to keep to myself, as closely as some would conceal a hidden joy. The world around me envies me as beautiful and happy—it is a deception of which I do not wish to rob them. That is why I appear gay, and dance; surely do I weep on the morrow, but I weep alone.'

"As she said these words, she threw upon me a glance inexpressibly sweet and confiding, and added—

"'You will come—come soon, will you not?'

"I carried her hand to my lips, and I retired.

"When I got home, I seemed in a dream. My windows looked upon hers; I remained all the day looking at them, and all the day they were closed and dark. I forgot everything for this woman; I slept not, I eat nothing. That evening I fell into a fever, the next morning I was delirious, and the next evening I was *dead!*"

"*Dead!*" cried his hearers.

"Dead!" answered the narrator, with a conviction in his voice which words alone cannot give; "dead as Fabian, the cast of whose dead face hangs from that wall!"

"Go on," whispered the others, holding their breath.

The hail still rattled against the windows, and the fire had so nearly died out, that they threw more wood on the feeble flame which penetrated the darkness of the studio and cast a faint light upon the pale face of him who told the story.

He resumed:—

"From that moment I felt nothing but a numbing chill, and a slight but still freezing motion. The latter was doubtless that of being put into the grave. I had been buried for some time—I do not exactly know how long, for there is no time-keeping in the grave—when I heard someone calling my name. I shook with cold and fear, without being able to answer. After a lapse of some moments, I was again called. I made an effort to speak, and then felt the bandage which wrapped me from head to foot. It was my shroud. At last, I managed feebly to articulate, 'Who calls?'

"''Tis I!' said a voice.

"'Who art thou?'

"'I! I! I!' was the answer; and the voice grew weaker, as if it was lost in the distance; or as if it was but the icy rustle of the trees.

"A third time my name sounded on my ears; but now. it seemed to run from tree to tree, as if it whistled in each dead branch; so that the entire cemetery repeated it with a dull sound. Then I heard a noise of wings, as if my name, pronounced in the silence, had suddenly awakened a troop of night-birds. My

29

hands, as if by some mysterious power, sought my face. In silence I undid the shroud which bound me, and tried to see. It seemed as if I had awakened from a long sleep. I was cold.

"I then recalled the dread fear which oppressed me, and the mournful images by which I was surrounded. The trees had no longer any leaves upon them, and seemed to stretch forth their bare branches like huge spectres! A single ray of moonlight which shone forth, showed me a long row of tombs, forming an horizon around me, and seeming like the steps which might lead to Heaven. All the vague voices of the night, which seemed to preside at my awakening, were full of terror.

"I turned my head, and sought for him who called me. *He* was seated at my side, watching me, his head leaning on his hands, and his face pregnant with a terrible look, and clothed with a horrible smile. Fear ran like an electric shock through me. 'Who art thou?' said I, with an endeavour to gather up all my strength; 'and why dost thou awaken me?'

"'To render you a service,' he answered.

"'Where am I?'

"'In the graveyard.'

"'Who art thou?'

"'A friend.'

"'Leave me to my sleep.' said I.

"'Listen!' cried he to me; 'dost thou remember aught of the earth?'

"'No.'

"'Dost thou regret anything?'

"'No.'

"'How long hast thou been asleep?'

"'I know not.'

"'I will tell you,' he said: 'Thou hast been dead two days; and the last word you uttered was the name of a woman, instead of that of the Lord. Therefore, if Satan wished to possess it, your soul belongs to him. Dost understand me?'

"'Yes,' I answered.

"'And dost thou wish to live?'

"'Who art thou who offerest me life?—art thou Satan?'

"'Satan, or not,' was the answer; 'will you live?'

"'Alone?'

"'No. You shall see *her*.'

"'When?'

"'This very night; and at her own house.'

"'I accept it,' cried I, trying to rise; 'what are thy conditions?'

"'I make none,' said the speaker, with a lurid smile. 'Do you believe that, from time to time, I am not capable of doing good? This very night *she* gives a ball: I will take you thither.'

"'Let us set out.'

"'Good!' cried Satan. He held forth his hand and dragged me from the place.

"You imagine that what I say was impossible. All that *I* say is, that I felt a penetrating cold, which froze all my limbs.

"'Now,' cried the fiend, 'follow me! You must understand that I cannot get out by the great gate—the porter will not suffer that. Once here, there is no retreat. Follow me, therefore: we will just go to your house, where you shall dress yourself; for you can hardly go to a ball in your present costume—especially as it is not a *bal masqué*. Mind and wrap yourself well up in your winding-sheet, for the nights are cold, and you may feel unpleasantly touched by it.'

"As he said this, Satan laughed malignantly; and I continued silently to walk after him.

"'I am sure,' continued he, 'that, in spite of the service I am doing you, you do not yet like me. You are always thus, you men—ungrateful to your friends. Not that I blame ingratitude; it is a vice upon which I pride myself, since I invented it myself; and I must say, that it is one most in vogue. But I do wish to see you a little more merry—it is the only thing I ask of you.'

"I answered not, but still followed my guide, white as a statue, and as cold. I was silent; but, at the pauses in the fiend's voice, I could hear my teeth chatter against each other, and my bones rattle in my body.

"'Shall we soon arrive?' said I, with effort.

"'Still impatient,' said my guide, sardonically. 'You must think her very beautiful?'

"'As an angel!' I cried.

"'Ah! my friend,' said he, with a laugh, 'one must confess that you have a want of delicacy in your answers. How can you talk to me of angels, knowing I have been one: in fact, I have done for you today somewhat more than an angel could have done. I excuse you, however; one must excuse a good deal to a man who has been dead upwards of two days. Besides, I am, as I have told you, very good-tempered today. There has happened in the world a few things which please me very much. I *did* think that men were degenerate; I absolutely fancied that they were getting virtuous. But, no; they are always the same—just the same as when first created. Well! today has been a rare day for me: I have seldom found things succeed so well as today. I have counted, since yesterday evening, six hundred and twenty-two suicides in France alone! Among them, there has, however, been more young men than old fellows, which is a pity, because they die without children, and are therefore a loss to me. Two thousand four hundred and forty-three in the whole of Europe.

"'The other parts of the world I do not count; *there*, I am like rich capitalists, who cannot count their gains. Twelve hundred judges, who have given false judgment: ordinarily I have more than this latter number. There are also twenty-seven cases of atheism—cases which gave me greater pleasure than all the rest put together. With these and others, you will find that they make together a rough aggregate of nearly three million souls in Europe alone! I have not reckoned petty crimes, such as theft, forgery, &c.; these are merely the farthings in the gross account. So you can easily calculate in what space of time the whole world will fall into my hands, at three millions of souls per day! I really fancy that I shall be obliged to enlarge my place of accommodation.'

"'I understand your triumph,' I muttered to myself, as I hastened onwards.

"'Indeed!' said Satan, with a sombre and melancholy air; 'do you fear me, then, since you see me face to face?—am I so repulsive? Let us reason a little: What would become of your world without me? It would die of spleen. It is I who invented gold-gambling! 'Tis I love! Business—'tis I! Thinking of these things, I cannot, for the life of me, understand the spite which you men seem to bear against me. Your poets, for instance, who keep talking of an ideal love, cannot understand that, in raving of the love which exalts, they point out the way to that which debases—that in seeking a Diana they manage to find an Aphrodite. Now look for instance to yourself; you have just arisen from the dead; you are yet as cold as a corpse; and yet you seek the embraces of love. You see evil survives death, and that a man who has lived a wicked life, would, if he were put to the proof, prefer an eternity of his own passions to an eternity of pure and heavenly happiness.'

"I interrupted him with—'Shall we soon get there?' for the horizon seemed to grow lighter every moment, and still we did not seem to advance an inch.

"'How impatient you are,' ejaculated the fiend, querulously: 'you must know that over the great gate of the cemetery there is a cross, and that that cross is a kind of barrier or custom-house to me. As I generally travel about for purposes which the cross forbids, I should be obliged to make the sign of it upon my forehead to pass it. Now, I am willing enough to carry on my own little peccadilloes, but the fiend himself revolts at sacrilege: so, as I have told you before, we can't pass there. But never mind that—follow me. I have promised to conduct you to a ball; and I will keep my word. *My* word,' added he, sardonically, 'is well known to be as good as my bond.'

"There was, in all this irony of the fiend, something so fatal, cold, and devilish, that almost each word which dropped from his mouth seemed to freeze me. Still, what I tell you I heard with these ears! I could not drag myself away from my strange companion.

"We continued to walk for some hundred feet, when we came to a wall, before which an accumulation of tombstones formed a kind of flight of steps. Satan placed his foot upon the first, and, without any remorse, strode upon the sacred memorials till he reached the top of the wall.

"'I hesitated; I was afraid to follow him: but he held out his hand to me, saying, 'There is not the slightest danger—you can step upon these paving-stones. They are those of some acquaintances of mine.'

"When I had reached the place where he stood, he suddenly asked me, 'Whether he should show me the town?' But I answered, 'No, no! let us move forward.' We therefore leapt down from the wall upon the ground.

"The moon seemed to veil herself before the bold looks of Satan. The night was cold. All the doors were closed, all the windows darkened, and the streets deserted. From their appearance, one would have imagined that, for a long time past no foot had traversed those silent streets. Everything around us bore a death-like aspect. It seemed as if, when day came, no one would open their doors; that no head, of woman or of child, would look out of those dark, dull windows; that no step would break the silence which fell, like a pall, upon all around. I seemed to be walking in a city which had been buried some ages. In truth, the town seemed to have beer depopulated, and the cemetery to have grown full.

"'Still we went forward, without hearing a murmur, or meeting even with a shadow. The street stretched for a long way across this fearful city of silence and repose. At last we reached my house.

"'You remember it?' said the fiend.

"'Yes,' replied I, sullenly, 'let us enter.'

"'First,' said he, 'we must open the door. It is I, by the way, who invented the science of opening doors without breaking them in. In fact, I have a second key to all doors and gates—with one exception—that of Paradise! '

"'We entered. The calm without continued within. It was horrible!

"I felt as in a dream: I did not breathe nor move. Imagine, if you can, yourselves entering your chambers, after having been dead for two days—finding everything in the same position in which it was during your illness, but wrapped in that dark gloom which death alone can give, and seeing all the objects arranged, never again to be disturbed by you! The only thing which seemed to have any motion in it which I had seen since I arose from the tomb, was a large clock, by the side of which a human being had ceased to exist, and which now ticked slowly on, counting the hours of my eternity, as it had the minutes of my life.

"I went to the mantelshelf; I lighted a wax candle to assure myself of the existence of everything; for all which surrounded me appeared so strange that I could not believe my senses. Every object was real: I saw before me the portrait of my mother, with the same smile upon her lips—smiling on me now in death—as it had before in life. I opened the books which I had read only some few days before my death; everything was the same. The only alteration was, that the linen had been removed from the bed, and that on each chest and drawer there was a seal. As for Satan, he was sitting down upon the tester of the bed, reading attentively the *Lives of the Saints*.

"'I passed before a cheval glass, and I saw myself from head to foot in my strange costume, wrapped in my winding-sheet, my face pale, my eyes heavy and dull; I began to doubt this life which an unknown power had returned to me. I placed my hand upon my heart, it did not beat—I carried my hand to my brow, my brow was cold as ice; so also was my chest: my pulse was, of course, as motionless as my heart. However, memory lived within me, and I could move about; the thought was horrible, my eyes and my brain were alone really alive.

"'What was yet more horrible was, that I could not detach my eyes from the glass, which gave back my figure, cold, pale, and frozen. Each movement of my lips was reflected by a ghastly and sinister smile. I could not quit my place, and I had no power to cry out.

"The time-piece gave out that dull sound which warns us

that it will soon strike; then it struck two o'clock. A few seconds after, the neighbouring church clock struck also, then another, and another, and all was again silent. By the reflection of the glass, I saw that the fiend had fallen comfortably to sleep over the volume he had tried to read.

"I turned round, and caught my reflection in another glass with that pale clearness which a single wax candle in a vast chamber gives; I seemed haunted by myself; fear reached its culminating point, and I cried out aloud. Satan awoke.

"'Look,' said he, not regarding my fear, 'how you men try to instil virtue into others. Here is this book, absolutely so nonsensical and dull, that I, who have not been to sleep for nearly six thousand years, am obliged to take a nap over it. How is this? Are you not yet ready?'

"'Look at me,' said I, mechanically.

"'Come, come,' answered my companion, ' break the seals, take your clothes, and plenty of gold—aplenty of gold. Tomorrow, when it is found out, justice will step in and condemn some poor devil for the robbery, and,' continued he, condescending for a moment to be vulgar, for the devil is always a gentleman, '*that will be a little bit of fat for me.*'

"I dressed myself in haste, but noticed every time that I touched my forehead or my bosom that they were still cold as ice. When ready, I looked at Satan.

"'Shall we see *her?*' said I.

"'In five minutes.'

"'And tomorrow, what then?'

"'Tomorrow,' said he, ' you may take yourself to your ordinary pursuits and to your common life. I do not do things by halves.'

"'Without conditions!'

"'Without any.'

"'Let us set out then,' I returned.

"We did so; in a few minutes we were before the house at which I had called some few days previously.

"'Let us go upstairs,' said my conductor. He did so. I recognized the grand staircase, the vestibule, the ante-chamber. The entrance of the saloon was crowded with people; the party was brilliant, the rooms seemed to glitter as it were with light, flowers, jewels, and beautiful women.

"When we entered they were dancing. I cannot tell how I felt, seeing all these things, and with yet the presence of the grave about me. I took Satan aside, and whispered to him, 'Where is she?'

"'In her *boudoir*,' he answered. I waited till the dance was finished; I then crossed the saloon. The huge mirrors, by the light of the chandeliers, reflected my pale and sombre figure, and I recognized that deathlike smile which had so frozen me. But *here* at least I was safe—*here* was no solitude, but a crowd of joyous people; no cemetery, but a ball-room—no tomb, but beauty, ravishing beauty. For one moment, dreaming of her for whom I came, I forgot *whence* I came.

"Arrived at the door of the *boudoir*, I glanced in, and saw her; there she sat, more beautiful than beauty's self—chaste as a statue of Diana. I stopped for an instant in an ecstasy: she was clothed in a dress of dazzling whiteness, with bare arms and shoulders; I thought I saw upon one of her arms the little red point where I had bled her; perhaps, however, this was more fancy than anything else. When I appeared she was surrounded by handsome young men, to whose vapid talk she did not, however, seem to listen; raising her beautiful eyes mechanically, she saw me, seemed to hesitate for a moment, and then, with a sweet smile, she quitted the rest and came to me.

"'You see,' said she, 'I am quite strong.' As she said this the orchestra again struck up; she continued 'And you can make proof of it if you wish; let us waltz together.' She then added some words to someone at her side; I looked towards him—it was Satan.

"'You have kept your word,' said I; 'I thank you for it, but this woman must become mine this very night.'

"'Thou shalt have her,' he said, coldly; 'but wipe your face before you dance, there is a worm crawling upon your cheek,' so saying he departed, leaving me more cold and ghastly than before. To restore my feelings, I pressed the arm of her for whom I had come from the grave, and thus I entered the ball-room with her.

"'It was one of those delicious entrancing waltzes where all those who surround us seem to disappear, and we see none but ourselves; so we waltzed with our eyes fixed on each other, till they seemed to make a language of their own. Hers seemed to say, 'I am young and beautiful, and to him who possesses me all the beauties of my heart and soul will be revealed.'

"Still the waltz went on; the measure ceased at last, and we were alone. She leaned upon my arm, and turned her fine eyes upon me with a look which seemed to say, 'I love you.'

"'I led her back into the saloon—it was deserted; she sat down, reclining on an ottoman, and turned her eyes to me, half closed, as if with love rather than fatigue. I leaned towards her: 'Ah,' said I, 'if you only knew how I love you.'

"'I know it,' she answered; 'I love you equally as well.'

"'I would give my soul,' said I, earnestly, 'to possess you as my bride.'

"The eyes of the lady lit up with a fire which resembled those of the fiend—their light seemed to enter into my soul, 'Listen,' she said, anxiously; 'in a few moments we shall be alone; that door leads to my chamber; wait till all are gone, and we will ratify the compact.'

"The door opened silently, and then shut upon me. I was alone in the chamber where first I had seen her: there was the same mysterious perfume, which one cannot describe. I glanced in the mirror, I was still as pale as ever; I heard the carriages which took up the guests, and departed one by one, until the last had disappeared, and the silence again became dreadful and mournful; I felt, little by little, step by step, my terrors return upon me. I dared not recall my former thoughts. I was astonished that my mistress never came. I counted the minutes till they seemed hours. I sat down and rested my elbows on my knees.

"Then I began to think of my mother, who at that moment was weeping for me—my mother to whom I had been all in life—to whom, alas, I had given but little, too little thought. Then came back the days of my childhood: I remembered that I had never had a moment's grief but that my mother had consoled it; and now, perhaps, when I was about to prepare for a crime, she was passing a vigil of tears and prayers in remembrance of me. The thought was fearful; I felt full of remorse—tears came into my eyes. I rose and looked at myself again in the glass: my eyes, before dull, seemed to brighten with resolution. I prayed within myself, and determined to rush from the present danger. I saw behind me a pale and motionless figure, it was my mistress; she had just entered the room. I rushed past her, through the half-opened door, and before I thought of anything else, I regained my own home.

"In the sanctity of that I remained in meditation and prayer; I was safe from the intrusion of the fiend who tempted me. Not so, however, were my thoughts. In the morning, which slowly dawned, the beauty to which I had so blindly bowed myself seemed to have regained its power. I forgot my good resolutions—I threw behind me my prayers—I again gave myself up to the passions which devoured me. I determined again to seek her. It was broad daylight when I went out of my room, but by the door-post a figure, formed, it seemed to me, of a dark vapour, stood and looked at me sardonically, I *felt* that it was the fiend, and I knew his power over me, and that he followed upon my steps.

"'The day was dark, dull, and cold; I walked carelessly, and, heedless of anything but of the purpose I had before me, I at last arrived.

"'At the moment I placed my foot upon the step, I saw an old man, pale and feeble, who was about to descend the flight of stairs which ran up to the door.

"'Who do you want, sir?' said the porter.

"'Madame P——,' I replied.

"'*Madame P——*,' returned he, with a look of astonishment, pointing out the old man at the time; 'that gentleman now inhabits this hotel; Madame P—— died three months ago.'

"I gave a loud cry, and fell forward senseless."

A silence fell upon the party who listened to this strange story: none dared for a few moments to break it. At last, one asked, "What further happened?" No one answered, and when they looked through the increasing gloom of the studio, they found that the narrator of the strange story had departed—none knew how, or when; nor did either of us ever again meet with the hero of the *Dead Man's Story*.

The Ghost's Forfeits

To serve them so!

Well it was enough to make a body swear: not but that swearing is wicked—awfully wicked; but then, to serve them so!

After Jemima Prettypuss had given up a husband—only she did not care about him—just to please *him*; after William, who had such fine talents—military talents,—at his expressed desire, had consented to lay them (the talents) aside, and had entered a counting-house, where he now was, at two pounds per week!—to serve them so!

After the presents Mrs. Schemer had made him,—the warm slippers, the jams and jellies, the real turtle soup in tin cases at two guineas a quart, the pineapples and grapes, the warm stockings, the guava jelly, the preserved ginger, the Scotch shortbread, the braces of pheasants and leashes of partridges—the latter sent to Mrs. Schemer by various friends and by her given up so generously for the good of Podgmore,—to serve her so! *This* was the return!

After Sir Paddington Buss, too, had consented to forego the very great difference in their rank and social position, and had danced attendance upon him at Brighton and at Cheltenham—at a dozen watering-places, indeed,—and had run the risk of meeting a bailiff in each place! After all this—after praising him at this club, and bragging about him at another, and involving himself more deeply when he ought to have been nursing his income on the Continent,—to serve *him* so!

And pretty Miss Plyable, too,—dear creature!—who played

so continually at whist (when she could not bear the game) simply because *he* was found of it; Miss Plyable who said she liked—ay, and wore too—brown bonnets, when blue only suited her complexion; Miss Plyable, who would have altered her taste in every particular at least ten times a day when she visited him; Kitty Plyable—she who pleased everybody, was voted charming by everybody, and had worked so hard to please him!

Who was it, too, who had abstained from playing on the *cornet-à-piston* because *he* liked quiet? That was little Fred Piston. Who showed him several wonderful tricks at cards and a peculiar stroke at billiards?—who but Captain Cushion. Who sent him those nice, delightful, soul-refreshing, desert-of-life-watering tracts? Of course that was the Reverend Matthew Ghoule. Who had consulted the welfare of his soul?—Ghoule. Who had begged him ten times a-day not to turn away from the plough?—Ghoule. Who studied the ease of his body?—all of them—but most particularly Mrs. Barbecue; for if anybody there had been especially pertinacious and attentive, that person was the widow Barbecue.

Yes, we are bound to say that all the relations of the deceased Podgmore had been excessively attentive in their inquiries after his health and welfare; had consulted him in every particular, and had, in that commendable way which people of this world use, played up to him remarkably well. They all deserved the fortune which he left; they had all been equally solicitous, equally attentive, except John Jibb and Miss Fanny Pinnock, who had both of them attended to their own inclinations, and had got on in the world in their own way.

Yet, see the result! They had been all treated alike; he had served them in a rascally way,—that was the term used by Sir Paddington Buss, Bart.; and Captain Cushion did not hesitate to use a much stronger term. Mrs. Barbecue was quite ready to endorse all those opinions, and as many more of the same sort as one could bring; and the company generally were not very much disposed. to defend the "defunct;" and with that cold term, which shall one day be used, dear reader, to me and to you, they let him rest.

Best! I promise you that the Reverend Mr. Ghoule, who was an authority on such matters, did not give him rest. He consigned him to a certain place where very little quietude and no rest at all can be expected; nor did any one of the relations defend him again, if we except Mr. John Jibb, who, with several sailor-like figures of speech—low expressions, Mrs. Barbecue called them—wretched, profane terms, said the Reverend Matthew Ghoule,—asserted that he would not find any fault with the old boy, and that perhaps—he wished he was—he was gone to heaven!

So that all parties invited expressly by Mr. Redwhacks, the lawyer, at the especial and dying request of the defunct, to spend Christmas at Coldblow House, agreed in abusing the deceased. He was to be buried on the day after. "Boxing-day!" cried Sir Paddington, profanely; and a suit of mournings a ring, and a Christmas dinner was, according to a certain memorandum left by deceased, to be provided for each. After dinner, so said this singular paper (but then Podgmore was always half mad),—

The Will

was to be read; but *they* knew the contents. Separately had Redwhacks informed them what each might expect; they were all cut off with the suits of mourning and the rings; and a hospital reckoned Podgmore amongst those who had benefited it by will.

★★★★★★

You may expect, therefore, that the party who upon Podgmore's death were all assembled in Coldblow House were not all silent. The conversation ran upon the acts and sayings of the deceased, and principally upon the disappointment which each had individually sustained. Miss Jemmy Prettypuss had said her say, and had invited everybody's confidence, whilst she freely gave them her own; and it was wonderful what that confidence produced. Each of the travellers in this weary world unpacked his or her troubles, and rang the changes of the Christian year with a dull burden of complaints. They were all, as Mr. John

Jibb grumbled forth in a song (for which Mr. Ghoule reproved him),

"United in a common cause,"

and their unanimity was wonderful; so, like the east wind which blew against the house—a sulky, gusty, and uncertain wind—and an open, draughty house it was, exposed on all sides—they grumbled, and sighed and moaned, whilst the cause of their complaints lay quiet upstairs.

To bring them all there to keep Christmas, when they should have been so far apart, almost in the four quarters of the globe, was a refinement of cruelty; and then for so small, so petty a purpose!

They were beginning again. Mrs. Barbecue led the charge in a startling way. Sir Paddington followed with a heavy rumble, and little Fred Piston squeaked out his wrath. The old wainscoted parlour echoed with it, and the blazing, crackling fire roared too, as it careered up the chimney. There was Christmas in its looks, and Christmas in the surging, sighing wind, though it was south-east and betokened rain and a breakup of the frost.

"Now," cried John Jibb, crossing his brawny arms backwards over the chair, and giving himself a great stretch, "don't belabour old dry bones any more. He's had enough, Mrs. Barbecue. Pray, Mr. Ghoule, stop them. His money has done more good than it would with any of us."

"What," cried Jemmy Prettypuss, pouting her lips, and glancing slyly at Mr. Ghoule, "more good than a new chapel, another 'Cave Adullam?'"

"Or than a carriage and establishment?" said Mrs. Schemer.

"Or paying my debts?" grumbled Sir Paddington Buss, Bart.

"Or than portioning off my daughters?" hissed Mrs. Barbecue.

"Or than making me rich and a patron of music?" whispered little Fred Piston.

"Or than buying me a German barony?" shouted Captain Cushion.

"Or than getting me a husband with a coronet ?" simpered Miss Kitty Plyable.

Hey day! how plain they were, all these wishes they had as yet scarcely confessed to themselves; but now the time for concealment was over—they had all played the same game, and had lost; they threw up their hands, therefore, and did not mind telling what cards they had held.

Miss Pinnock alone said nothing, but elevated her pretty eyebrows, and turned up a very nicely-shaped nose in a marked manner, just as Mr. Ghoule was about to *improve* the occasion, and to *prove* Mr. Podgmore a "son of wrath." John Jibb noticed it, and stretched himself once more, in such a sailor-like fashion that he made the chair crack again.

"Mr. Jibb," cried Mr. Redwhacks, "do not damage the property of the testator."

"The testator be——" said Captain Cushion.

"He no doubt will be," answered the reverend gentleman, politely interrupting the captain, so that the sentence was not completed.

"Oh, burn his old chairs, burn them!" cried Mrs. Barbecue, who had any time these ten years looked upon them as her own, and had hitherto treated them tenderly.

"Oh, Mrs. Barbecue!" giggled Miss Pinnock, merrily, "why not long ago you scolded me for sitting down suddenly on them."

"Hold your tongue, miss!" cried the old lady, "and don't try to curry favour with John there, although he is a relation."

Miss Fanny Pinnock blushed deeply at this, and John told his aunt that it was too bad, and proposed that, as it was Christmas Eve, they should, as they had met together in a very extraordinary manner, amuse themselves with some game.

"A game!" cried everybody aghast, glancing at their black clothes, and then at the portrait of the late owner of the house, which hung opposite the fire, looking down upon the little party with a curious supervision.

"No!" cried Mrs. Schemer, "little as I respected the deceased, little as I have cause to respect him, still I will not, with him in the house."

"*Pray, do not mind ME,*" said a voice which they all knew. It was the voice of Podgmore, and as they looked round, there stood behind them, descended from his picture, Podgmore himself!

They did not shriek. They did that which the reader would do if he were to see a ghost. They sat quite still, nearly stupefied. In some manner the eyes of the ghost seemed to look into the soul of each, and he wished them, with a sinister turn of countenance, "a merry Christmas," and bade them welcome.

"And now," he said, "since you are met here, pray favour me by following out this excellent gentleman's suggestion and playing at some game. You, Mr. John Jibb," said the horrid old ghost, boring that gentleman right through with his keen eyes, "you were about to propose—"

"Blind-man's-buff," said the unfortunate Jibb, who appeared to be in a weak state, and whose memory had reverted to the time when he believed in ghosts—his schoolboy days.

"And a very good game, too," answered the defunct Podgmore, rubbing his marble-cold hands, and polishing the blue nails, just as if he could warm them.

Now the truth is, that Mr. Jibb had been so bored and hurt, and thoroughly upset, by that which he politely termed the "clack" of the women, that he was about to say "Chess," or "Draughts," or "Dominoes"—not liking, as a reverend gent was there, to mention "Cards"—especially as they had met for such a melancholy occasion. But the ghost puzzled him. How often had he declared that he did not believe in spirits! How often had he laughed at the superstitions of sailors! And now there stood the ghost of Podgmore before him.

The rest of the company felt very little better. Sir Paddington stood fanning himself; Mrs. Barbecue had fainted; the Rev. Mr. Ghoule was muttering an exorcism; and the captain was swearing softly to himself, oaths being that kind of adjuration which came most naturally to him. Not one of them could take his eyes from the ghost, and he took care to fix his upon the whole party.

"Well," said he at last, opening a mouth of which the lips were blue, and which, when opened, was as black as a coal-cellar; "well, why don't you begin? Stay a moment—I'll be the blind man."

Every one of them seemed glad enough at that; each thought to escape those dreadful eyes, which, without brightness or spec-ulation, but with that kind of glaze upon them which glass ac-quires by being buried long in the earth—yet seemed to transfix them.

In a moment the ghost had blinded those eyes, which he did very cleverly by wrapping his shroud round his head; and in another moment he was after them.

Yes, after them he was!—round the tables, over the chairs, behind the screen, in the comers, behind the curtains, in the cupboards, at the top of the sofa—everywhere in fact. The rev-erend gentleman lay down under the table; Mrs. Barbecue put herself atop of the piano, and lay still. They all tried the door, but that was bolted and locked outside. They scampered and ran, bumped against each other, shrieked, groaned, and cried—all to escape that dreadful, horrible ghost, who, with a shroud over his head, and extended claws, came after them in that terrible game of blind-man's-buff.

But he caught them all. He picked up the Rev. Ghoule first, and extracted a toothpick from him as a forfeit; next, he found Captain Cushion, and from him he got a false die; after him came Miss Plyable, who gave up a scent-bottle; then Sir Paddington, who delivered his pencil-case; then Mrs. Barbecue, from whose time-honoured head he snatched a front; then Mr. John Jibb, who presented the ghost with a boatswain's whistle; after him, Mr. Fred Piston, who had nothing but a battered sixpence about him; and, finally, Susan Schemer and Miss Pinnock, who, both screaming violently, ran into each other's arms and were caught easily, and from them he took a little port-*monnaie* and a lace-edged pocket-handkerchief; and, last of all. Miss Jemmy Prettypuss, from whom he took a letter from a certain sweetheart, which she always carried with her.

After all these forfeits were collected, and the company, with their rich mourning, their frightened looks, and scared minds, had, half out of breath, sat down, the ghost himself rested demurely in his arm-chair, and began solemnly and deliberately to "cry" them.

The amazement of the company cannot be described; but, as Podgmore was always eccentric, why should not his ghost be so too? The shroud still rested upon his brow, and his eyes were yet hidden from those of his guests and playmates, when, in a sepulchral voice, the animated spirit uttered:—

"Here's a pretty thing, and a very pretty thing, and what is the owner of this pretty thing to do?"

No one answered; so the mocking voice of Podgmore, so like his living tones, yet so unlike them, repeated the question, as he twirled and twisted the brown false hair front of Mrs. Barbecue. The wretched woman awoke to her sense of degradation, and made a snatch at it; but the mocking ghost still held it, as he said (and his tones grew solemn and deep):—

"She is to leave off all falseness, all self-seeking, of which her life has been one tissue; she is to retire to her own street in town, never to retail a word more of scandal, and to try to live charitably with her neighbours as an honest woman should; for charity and honesty consist not entirely in alms-giving, nor in refraining from picking and stealing, but also in affection to all, and in a noble endeavour to retail no ill word of any living thing. Go, then, old woman!" said the voice, "clothe the gray honours of thy head with falseness no longer."

Mrs. Barbecue answered with a groan, and adjusted her head-dress, when another forfeit was cried, and the "Bart." started forward to claim it.

"Go, sir," said the spirit, "go! and for your punishment you are condemned to do some kind of work, either of the head or hand; but work it must be. As you do nothings it is plain that, in the economy of nature, someone must work for you; whilst you, in your pride of place, of birth, rank, and state, scorn the humble means of your existence, thinking yourself better than the rest of humanity. Go to, frivolous and stupid man,—go to; mend your ways—or, when these despised creatures awake, there will be for you and your class a heavy day of reckoning. You are condemned, therefore, for the rest of your days to do something useful for society."

As the last words left the cavernous mouth of the ghost. Sir Paddington's tooth-pick was flirted across the room into its owner's face, and whilst the "Bart." bemoaned his hard fate, the skinny hand was again held up, and the forfeit of Miss Jemmy Prettypuss exposed to view.

"As for you, madam, I condemn you to your dearest wishes," said Podgmore. "Marry a man of rank—marry the baronet. You have been angling, smirking, ogling, throwing out baits innumerable for many years; you want a title—so become that gentleman's lady. Equally frivolous, and equally selfish, you will henceforth punish each other. What to you. Miss Prettypuss, were the hearts of a dozen honest, earnest fellows, if they had no money? What for you were the hopes and love, the pangs and sorrows, of a dozen girls whose lovers you flirted with and cast off? The whole aim of your being was selfishly to excite attention, to play your own game, caring little who lost, so that you won."

Miss Jemmy, with this rebuke, retired, and sat down at the side of the baronet, and the next forfeit was cried. It was a false die, heavier on one face than on another.

"This pretty thing," said the ghost with deep mockery, "belongs to Captain Cushion. Come hither, captain; it is false and uneven as your way in life; but false as it is, and as you are, you are not worse in using it than many of these around you, who throw falsely in the game of life, and prefer fortune-hunting and a thousand other by-ways of making or acquiring money, to honest industry. Your punishment, therefore, shall be no heavier than theirs. You must renounce your swearing, your free living, and your evil ways, and ever attendant upon our friend the Bev. Matthew Ghoule, you must listen to his discourses and read his tracts, till you fall in love with his doctrines, and reform. That you may at once begin, I here make you a present of a small instalment of tracts."

And to the captain's dismay, the spirit took from its pocket a bundle of the identical papers so kindly presented to it in its body by the Rev. Mr. Ghoule.

"As for thee, sir," cried the ghost, exhibiting the clergyman's forfeit, "thou, who in thy endeavours after a religious life, hast never forgotten religion; who preferrest poverty to riches, and who attendest upon the poor equally well with the rich,"—the clergyman felt the bitter satire and blushed,—"who exalt-est charity by constant bickerings, who condemnest all except thyself; and never to the young and generous hast yet presented the most beautiful and touching portion of Christianity—its universal love and forbearance; but with a keen eye to every advantage, hast sought, by guile and wile, to make the best of this world, if not of the next—thou art condemned to preach, without a congregation, without reporters, notices, or praise, to this fellow-sinner, Captain Cushion, till he is wholly reformed."

Mr. Ghoule gave a heavy and hopeless groan, and with a look of intense disgust at the captain, sat down by his side.

Mr. Fred Piston, whose forfeit was next displayed, came up for judgment in company with Kitty Plyable. The ghost gave a grim smile as he looked upon them. "Your punishment con-sists," he cried, "in marrying each other, and by the time you have learned to love, your atonement will be complete; frivolous and aimless creatures!—but not so frivolous but that you could stalk an old man down, and truckle to him for his fortune.

"And you, Mrs. Susan Schemer," he continued, "you, whose whole idea seems to have been that of gratifying selfishness,—you, whose aim in life always centred in your own little person, who loved your very husband and children but as a portion of that precious body,—your punishment shall be, that in all your wishes you shall be crossed and defeated; till, by continued dis-appointment, you learn that a straightforward course is not only much better, but in the long run is more successful, than a devious one; and that honesty is not more surely the best policy, than that a sacrifice of *self* is the most generous, and often the most prudent, action in one's life.

There now remained only two of the party whose forfeits were uncried; these were Mr. John Jibb and Miss Fanny Pinnock. They had been the most wayward of all whilst Podgmore lived, and had endeavoured less than any to please him; but whilst others were waiting for the dead man's shoes, followed a plan, which is not, thank Heaven, yet exploded in England, and set resolutely to work to carve out a fortune for themselves.

The ghost, when he came to these two, took the boatswain's silver whistle in one hand and a lace-edged pocket-handkerchief in the other; and having blown down the former, whereby he produced of course merely the ghost of a whistle, he cried, for the last time, "Here are two pretty things, two very pretty things; now, what shall be done to the owners of these two pretty things?"

The same sad, dreary, weary silence ensued; and the ghost proceeded, answering his own question:—

"They shall go, as soon as their period of mourning hath expired, from this place to the church, there to be married, and to live afterwards faithfully and happily together; for, as from the marriage of some in this world, punishment springs, so from the union of others we may date their true happiness. Let it be so with you in future, Mr. and Mrs. John Jibb. You have been single-hearted to the world; you will, therefore, be so to each other; and that no ills may spring from poverty to interrupt your happiness, I here present you with a codicil to the will of the late Podgmore, which bestows upon each of you one hundred pounds a year. The remainder of his fortune he has thought best to bestow elsewhere."

When the ghost mentioned money, it was observed, by those who had presence of mind enough to watch him, that his countenance grew more human. Such an effect has the all-potent name of gold upon any of those who are or have been denizens of this world. Upon the disappointed fortune-hunters, too, it had a monstrous effect: Mrs. Barbecue shrieked forth that the sum was mean and paltry, the "Bart." jabbered inaudibly, the captain swore a great oath, and the parson looked up inquiringly.

But the most remarkable effect of all, was that which gold never fails to have; or at least one similar to it. All turned round upon the couple, and, with an ill-concealed wish to abuse them, began to wish them joy and to flatter them. From these, however, we must except Mrs. Susan Schemer, who, her hopes being much deeper than the rest, was so perturbed by their total destruction and rude uprooting, that she went into what is known as "kicking hysterics," from which fit the shins of the parson suffered.

This occasioned some diversion; everyone was anxious to bring her to, and when the hubbub was over, they turned round to the chair in which they had seen the deceased sitting, and found that piece of furniture corporeally occupied by Mr. Redwhacks, the lawyer. They then perceived that the fire had nearly died out, that the candles had burnt to the sockets, and that the hands of the dismal old clock, the pendulum of which had, all through the horrible scene, been "beating out the little lives of men," pointed to the magic hour of one.

The only thing which really remained, in proof of this extraordinary visitation, was the codicil to the will, in the hands of Mr. John Jibb, requesting him to marry his cousin, and bequeathing them the sums aforesaid.

★★★★★★

—No, no, no! I insist upon it. I am not going to make anything like a natural end to this story. In my opinion, and in that of the narratrix of the story to me, no, less than Mrs. John Jibb *née* Pinnock, it *was* a real GHOST; and, like a good spirit, taught lessons worth the teaching. And so my friends will do well to learn some little—very little perhaps—from me; for, oh! remember what a kindly, holy, joyous season it is, refreshing a whole year of bitterness with most of us, if we but properly remember the cause we keep it sacred for, and think that so many hundreds of years ago, a little Child was born, from whose holy teachings all kindliness and Christian love arose. But yet—ah me! How many upon this blessed Christmas time, will forget the pleasant tidings of peace and goodwill, and forgetfulness of self; and will but be guided by money-seeking and self-interest, even as to the puddings which they eat, and the mince-pies which they chronicle as devoured.

From all such. Heaven defend us. No kindly reader of this book will do so; but will make a Christmas in other hearts than his own—so shall no ghost rise to cry him

FORFEITS!

The Black Madonna

(A Phantom Story, Adapted From Alphonse Karr)

I must beg two thousand three hundred and sixty-five pardons from my Protestant readers for introducing to them a story of great beauty. I know that they will not forgive me for it; for it will touch them, and exhibit Catholic faith to them so prettily and sweetly, that the young ladies will be wishing to become *nonnettes*, and the dear young mothers will be singing hymns to the Virgin. *Mais que voulez-vous?*

Reading M. Alphonse the other day, I was so touched with the story that I turned it into English—not as Phillips did a Persian ode—for half a crown, but to please one of the dearest ladies in England. She was charmed; so was I. I have Protestantized it as much as I could, so that the thunders of the —— and the —— should not fall upon my book!

Pish! what honest reader will like it the less. Faith is of no country, nay, nor of any one singular church. 'Tis with them and with us; with black Sambo at a camp meeting; with old Aunt Bridget at a revival; with Don Francisco in his lonely cell. That I do not like Mariolatry Heaven knows; but I cannot condemn a lost mother who, in her wild grief, turns aside her prayers to the Almighty, to address them to the most lone Mother that the world ever knew.

★★★★★★

When you go to Chartrs, or, rather, when you pass that place after having traversed the monotonous and vast plains of Beauce, it may happen that, to enliven your spirits, you have to await for three hours the diligence which should meet that by which you came from Paris. Railways will soon put an end to this nuisance, but, at present, should it happen, and if, in the midst of the bad temper which the above announcement (made with the coolest possible manner by the superintendant of the *messageries*) is sure to throw you, you should stamp and turn round, and, in so doing, catch a glimpse through the trees of the two clock-towers of the cathedral, I congratulate you. That glimpse will repay the waiting and the ill-temper.

I am going to tell a story—not to give any description of the cathedral. But, in addition to its architecture, and to the extraordinary length of nave, it also possesses, more than any church which I have seen, that quality which inspires at once a feeling of mysticism and of ardent devotion. The building, which is so pierced and fretted that it admits light like a piece of lace-work, is remarkable for the beauty, the size, and the painted glass of its windows; for the carving which surrounds the nave; and for its mosaic pavement, the windings of which are such that they can be traced by the devout for many a mile without going out of the cathedral—a pilgrimage which is often performed, and to which are attached certain indulgences. But that which I have more immediately to speak of is, that there is a chapel in the cathedral, wherein, night and day, waxen lights are burning before the figure of a *Black Madonna* richly clothed and sparkling with precious stones. She is called "Our Lady of Miracles," and the ornaments with which she is adorned are each a testimony of gratitude from those who have had recourse to her intercession.

Many years ago, there lived at Chartres a young widow, who, rejecting all offers of a second match, devoted the remainder of her youth and beauty to a son, upon whom also rested all that love winch she once gave to her husband. The careful tending of his mother, and of Dame Nature herself, had made this boy the envy of other mothers and the pride of his own; and he was, indeed, an object of love and envy—healthful, well-made, and handsome, and of a tender and noble physiognomy which seemed to promise both goodness and greatness for the future.

Among other qualities with which this boy was endowed, was a voice as pure and angelic as ever had been heard; and his mother taught him some sacred songs breathing forth love and filial affection, which, when he sang them, used, from their very sweetness, to draw tears, not only from the eyes of his mother, but also from those of the few friends who remained to her.

So it happened that when the month of December came round, the Bishop of Chartres himself, who had heard of the fame of this little fellow's singing, came to ask the widow to let her son sing at the most solemn feast of the Church; and the good bishop said that his beauty, the openness of his countenance, the sweetness and goodness of his nature, and the sweet purity of his voice, in which he so nearly approached the angels, could not but be pleasing to the Virgin herself, and could not fail to touch the hearts of the children, and the mothers, who would also assist at the *fête*.

On the feast-day, therefore, the widow, having granted the request, forgot for a while the seclusion she had lived in; laid aside her mourning, which she had ever worn since her husband died, and almost reassumed the airs of a young and pretty woman as she prepared herself and her son for the ceremony.

After the procession had stopped before the altar of the Virgin, and whilst the nave was filled with the solemn pealing of the organ, the choir children ceased for a moment from casting flowers upon the altar, and the widow's son, clothed in a white tunic, with his long hair falling on his shoulders, bound round with a blue fillet, advanced from the midst of a crowd of boys of his own age. He knelt before the altar of the Virgin, and then raised his fine blue eyes, sparkling with emotion, to the shrine. Then it was, when the congregation scarcely breathed, and all were silent in holy expectation, that the pure, solemn, angel voice of the boy broke forth:—

Regina coeli, Iaetare, alleluia,
Quin quem meruisti portare, alleluia.

His mother, hearing the voice of her boy, wept in happiness, and when he came to the end of the hymn,

Gaudere et laetare, O Virgo Maria!

the choir children cast upon him the winter roses which they had in their baskets, and covered him with a perfumed cloud; but when that cloud had disappeared, there was nothing beneath the flowers—the boy had vanished!

Notwithstanding that every effort was made, it was impossible to find him. His mother and her friends traversed the town—the magistrates searched everywhere—but without success. The poor widow then refused to see any one; she passed her days in kneeling down and praying upon the pavement where she had last seen her son, and her nights in weeping, or in dreaming, when sleep had closed her eyes, that she saw her little boy far up in the rosy clouds of heaven, singing in the midst of the choir of angels.

Misfortune often follows misfortune as constantly as the waves break upon the shore—so it was with the widow. The family of her husband, having never consented to his marriage, sued her for all the property which she held, as executrix of her husband's estate, for her son; and, after a tedious law-suit, she was completely ruined. The poor creature paid but little attention to this; her whole heart and affection had gone with her husband and son, and she heeded nothing upon earth. She lived poorly upon the sale of some jewels which remained to her, and never missed a day but she went and prayed before the altar of the Lord.

In a short time her stock was exhausted, and she had nothing to live upon. She applied to the relations of her husband, but they answered her with scorn and with reproaches; and, of all her property, there now only remained the portraits of her husband and son, but she would have parted with life rather than have sold them. She at last dragged herself to the cathedral, and there knelt down upon the pavement and commenced her prayers, hoping that her hunger—for she had eaten nothing for two days—might kill her, and that she should from that spot be united to her son.

In spite of herself, of her cares, and her sorrows, she was attracted by the bustle and preparations which were going on in the church. They were decorating it with green branches and with flowers, and they dressed with unusual attention the altar of the Saviour. It was Christmas Day—the anniversary of that upon which she had lost her son. She blessed Heaven that she was about to die upon the self-same day—and then she knelt down in a corner and covered her head with her widow's veil.

Some persons in the cathedral recognized her, but durst not disturb her pious devotion,; they, therefore, only talked quietly to each other about her misfortunes, and about the rumour which accused the relations of her husband of having made away with the boy, so that they might gain his fortune.

The ceremony commenced. The poor widow ceased to weep, and, with an inexpressible joy, she felt herself grow fainter and fainter as it proceeded.

The procession was formed as before; then it stopped before the chapel of the Virgin; then the organ filled the whole church with a celestial harmony; clouds of incense floated upwards, and flowers covered the mosaic pavement of the church. There was a moment of silence, during which the sighs of the poor widow could be heard.

All eyes were turned towards her, and they saw her dying, pale, poverty-stricken, and in rags, whom but a year before they had seen so beautiful and so happy. Suddenly, in the midst of the silence, a voice broke forth, pure and clear, like that of an angel, which sang—

Regina coeli, laetare, alleluia.
Quia quem meruisti portare, alleluia,
Resurrexit, sicut dixit, alleluia.

The widow fell to the ground fainting, and all near her knelt down, weeping; for the angel which sang was none other than the little boy, her son—who, clothed in his white tunic, with his fair hair falling upon his shoulders, bound round his forehead with the blue fillet, stood upon the very stone whence he had disappeared.

The mother crept on her knees to him, and held him with all her strength, fearing that he would again vanish. The children of the choir covered both mother and child with a shower of roses: and, in the midst of the assembly, the bishop, applying to the widow the words of the hymn which the boy had sung, said, in a loud and solemn voice:

O rejoice!
For he thou barest in thy bosom lives
And is arisen!

The organ then again pealed forth, and never did so numerous a congregation pray with so much fervour and faith!

✦✦✦✦✦✦

The widow's son related what had occurred to him, as a dream which had left few traces in his mind. He remembered only the countenance of a female, more beautiful in his eyes than even his mother, although her face was *black*, who had nourished him with a delicious honey; and also that he had mingled his voice with a choir more harmonious and divine than those of earth.

So the story is, that when they dug beneath the stone whence the little chorister had vanished, they found that which now adorns the cathedral—the statue of the "Black Madonna!"

The Oxford Ghost

"Boodle, sing a song!"

I addressed the obese individual of that name, the "capital B." as he delighted to be called, in the midst of a festive party. I always make a point thereat of asking the wrong man to do the right thing; it gives such a blaze of triumph to the capable if you show up the incapable. It makes the giant look taller, the strong man stronger. I ask the clown to dance, the dull man to make a joke, the fellow who should only be trusted with a spoon to carve a chicken! Boodle could no more sing than a crow.

"Sing a song!" he answered, with the voice of a trombone; "I would as soon swallow the poker. I am not a bashful man; but I am past singing—if ever indeed I was fit for it, and I do not much think that I ever was. I never sang in my life but I felt ashamed of myself for doing so. Some people tune away, vociferating pleasantly, watching the flies on the ceiling, with an air about them which tells anyone how cleverly they think they do it. They like it, I suppose; but as for myself, I never in all my life sang but I felt uneasy for at least three weeks afterwards. The last time I attempted anything of the sort was when I went to a whitebait dinner; and do you know that I could not look any of my friends in the face for three weeks afterwards. Pleasant that, was it not? Sing! no, I'll die the death of a martyr first!"

"Then you will do something to amuse the party. A Christmas party comes but once a year—is sacred to old feelings, old superstitions, old stories, old songs, old loves, old fancies, and old remembrances. Thank Heaven for Christmas!"

"Amen!" said the priest, piously.

"You have been," said the soldier of the party, carefully caressing his whiskers—"you have been out in the world a great deal, sir?"

"Oh yes," answered my uncle, "out a good deal—out of my reckoning sometimes, out of spirits very often, out of sorts as well—very seldom, till I grew rather wiser, out of debt; and when I was young, I must confess it, what with dancing at parties with pretty girls, and staying late at bachelors' rooms—very often 'out' of nights."

"In those nocturnal rambles did you ever see a ghost?"

"Well," answered my uncle, "I can't say that I did, and I can't say that I did not. I am in a state of perplexity between the two. To my dying day, there is a point which I can never solve; and I don't believe I shall either—no, not if I live to be eighty. It was about Christmas time too."

"How was it, then?"

"Why, thus. I was in my younger days a 'bagman.' Why they called us 'bagmen' I don't know, nor do I care. Your aunt did; she used to be preciously wild about it. But so long as I pleased my customers and got orders for the house of which I am now the head, what cared I? I dare say that the young fellows who look to inherit my sovereigns will not think them less heavy because they were earned by a 'bagman.' I would rather be called a bagman than a commercial gent—'commercials' they call them now that they are whisked about from place to place in railway-carriages. Ah! mine were the days; when I travelled I did the thing like a gentleman, with my black-bodied gig and yellow wheels, and fast-trotting mare, I used to astonish the country people, and there was not a barmaid along the road, within forty miles of London, who had not made love to me after her fashion; but then I had metal more attractive in London.

"Well, I was going what I called the Midland circuit, in this very same gig, driving this very same mare. It was just after Thurtell cut Wearers throat, and a melancholy time it was. The country papers were full of murders; and every passenger on the road looked sharply into the faces of those whom he met, and thought every other person a highwayman. As for me, I put a couple of good double-barrelled pistols close to me in the gig, buttoned my coat round me, and determined to take my chance.

"I was in the tobacco trade then, as now,—p'raps so many people did not smoke as now,—p'raps they did; but at any rate cigars and tobacco were higher in price; and we made such a good thing of it, that no one could afford to keep a traveller from taking orders, especially just about Christmas time, when I was closing up the orders for the old year and getting fresh in for the new.

"Well, I was down in Oxfordshire, travelling northward, and I got to Oxford a few days before Christmas. When I got there I found a letter from the governors, stating that at about twenty miles north a bill would be due, and would be paid at the bank there, upon the day after Christmas Day. I knew they were in want of money, and I quite understood that my orders were imperative that I should be ready to present the bill when due. I wanted to get home amazingly; but what was to be done? The bill *must* be presented, and so there was an end of it.

"Sure enough I stayed in Oxford to eat my Christmas dinner. I went to church, and heard the cathedral service in the morning, and joined in the Christmas hymn. I looked hard at the melancholy old fellows—the few, very few, who were left in the colleges upon that day. I thought how lonely must their life be; and before I went to dinner I walked into two or three of the colleges, and marked one or two solitary lights in the windows of some of the quadrangles, and thought, almost with tears in my eyes, of the poor solitary scholars, the reading men, who were there alone with their books upon Christmas Day.

"I made myself thoroughly miserable about them, I can tell you. They might have rare puddings in the hall, and fine beef, I dare say; but the poor sizar or servitor (one's Oxford and t'other Cambridge, I don't know which—they are the same thing in spirit) sat there by his twinkling candle, thinking, I'll be bound, of Christmas Day at home.

"I was so melancholy and depressed with these thoughts, that it came into my head that the best thing I could do was to drive them away, or else I knew that I should spoil my dinner. I therefore whistled the fag-end of a tune; it was, 'Begone, dull care,' then fashionable, I think, and began my journey towards the White Hart. Mine was not to be a solitary dinner. Groggins, an enterprising young fellow in the wine trade—he has chalk atones on his fingers, a large fortune, and occasional fits of *delirium tremens* now—was to be my companion; and after dinner the landlord was to come up, and to bear his part in a song, and in a bowl of punchy which, in honour of its being Christmas, he had, time out of mind, provided for us bagmen.

"Well, I was just stepping out of the quad at Corpus, turning round my head to look at the solitary twinkling light of one poor devil in the corner, when who should I run against but a collegian. He was a tall, thin, melancholy man, with a torn gown, a very seedy square cap—things which then, as now, were honourable; and from the state of these things I knew him to be learned. He was making towards the light I was looking at, when I ran bump against him. He did not hurt me—I was a stout fellow then; but I must have given him an awkward knock, for I sent him flying yards away. He was as polite as Chesterfield, for he capped to me at once and bowed, and asked my pardon for his awkwardness. *That* told me that he was a poor student, a sizar. If he had been a gentleman commoner or a nobleman, he would have sworn at me like a bagman.

"Your awkwardness, sir?" cried I; "upon my word it was mine, and mine alone; and to apologize more substantially for it, may I be so bold as to wish you a Merry Christmas?"

"I said this in my jolliest voice, and took off my hat as I said it.

The collegian gave a sigh, as he answered, "A Merry Christmas—I wish one to you, sir."

"That sigh troubled me so much, that my mind was made up what to do at once. I quite pitied the student, and putting out my hand, took his—a long, thin, cold, consumptive hand it was—and shook it. 'Come, sir,' said I, 'do me the favour, if you have no better invitation, to come and dine with me at the White Hart; I am no scholar myself, and hope I don't offend you; I mean it in goodwill; a bottle of old port, a cut from the breast of a turkey, and a piece of beef, will do neither of us harm I will wager.' Here I fell to whistling 'The roast beef of Old England,' for want of filling up the pause in a better way,

"The student smiled in a faint shadowy way at my manner, and without a pause accepted the invitation.

"When I had got him, I felt somehow awkward, and did not know what to do with him. Here was a gentleman and a scholar accepting the invitation of a 'bagman.' How should I make him jolly? Would my rude mirth and town stories please him? Would he care to know the maker's price of the weed? I was so fat and burly—he so long, thin, and shadowy; I so untaught, he so learned; I knew this by his air, his manner, his walk. I felt at the same time awkward and proud, frightened and rejoiced, at my guest's presence.

"Presently the sound of Christmas bells came upon the air; so jubilant, ringing, thronging, hurrying through the air; tumbling over each other in their hurry to get through the belfry bars, and carrying so much good fellowship with them, that I felt quite ashamed of my pride. 'Eighteen hundred and twenty years ago,' thought I; 'there was no pride about the invitation given then. It *is* a holy season, and the best way to keep it holy is to behave naturally and kindly, and to put my pride in my pocket. After all, I am not sure that the student will not be very glad to dine with me.'

"These thoughts flashed through my brain in a minute. I had scarcely gathered up my thoughts, when, through the ringing of the bells, I heard the voice of my acquaintance propose that he should run to his rooms and change his dress; but I, looking at my watch, and not sorry at walking with a 'gown,' took his arm within mine, and declaring that not a moment was to be lost, set out for the White Hart.

"The landlord looked surprised at me and my guest: what was more, the 'boots'—who, with a shining face, and hair combed straight upon his forehead, stood at the door, partly in expectation of a Christmas-box, and partly to greet his old friends—absolutely did not recognize the student. I should tell you that 'boots' was an old boots, and that his peculiar pride and fame lay in the fact that he positively could remember the faces of every one of the members of the colleges; and that upon consulting him upon any point in that way, he was never found to trip.

"Well, we went up into the great room of the inn. The landlord had drawn the screen round the table, enclosing the fire, and endeavoured to take away from the vastness of the room. There was a four-branch candlestick, with wax candles, but they did not seem to me to give much light. The very fire on the hearth, which was roaring up the huge chimney when we came in, I fancied to smoulder down all of a sudden, and the wax candles actually to want snuffing. A letter, with a great vulgar commercial seal, lay upon the table. It was from my intended companion Tom Groggins, who wrote to say he had been invited to a Christmas dinner, at a tradesman's upon whom he had called for orders, and finished by a 'P.S.—Two of the daughters sing like angels!'

"I wished the daughters had been anywhere else. I depended upon Tom Groggins's cheerful voice and air. I absolutely felt my spirit sinking. 'I am very sorry, sir,' said I to the student; 'but positively I shall have to do all the honours myself. My friend has disappointed me, and I have got no vice.'

"'No what?' queried the student.

"'No vice, no gentleman to support me!'

"'Oh, that is all!' cried he, gaily; 'I did not quite take you at first. Oh, never mind, I'll be your vice—I'll support you.' Here he took off his cap, disclosing a beautifully high pale forehead, down the very centre of which the short curly crisp hair grew in a peak, allowing me to notice temples which were as white and polished as the cicatrice of a burn; just as if, indeed,—as if two horns had been cut off, and the wounds cauterised.

"He sat down with great alacrity, and the first course, a boiled turkey, having been placed on the table, I sat down too, and proposed to say grace, which I never omit upon Christmas Day. 'Stop,' cried the student, '*I* belong to the clerical profession; I am a clerk, though not in orders; I'll say grace; do you say it in English?'

"'Of course I do,' I returned.

"'Ah,' he exclaimed, '*I* say it in Latin—an old form, you know.'

"'Say on, then,' I answered; 'no matter what the form be, I can think, though I am no scholar.'

"' Good,' returned the student, bending down his head, so that the white temples glistened in the light. He then uttered very heartily a few words, which *he* said were the grace, but which I thought, strangely enough, sounded like an imprecation.

"We fell to, but not with that hearty goodwill which one should when at a Christmas dinner. There is something peculiarly Christian-like and jolly in eating; at least, so I think. Men eat variously, to be sure; some spread about their victuals over their plates, then glower over them, and then devour them. Some men eat ravenously, like wolves; others daintily, like pretty ladies; some men nibble, others gobble and bolt. My friend did not do either. The victuals seemed to glide and slide from the edge of his plate to his knife and fork, and thence to his mouth, with an ease and agility which astonished and confounded me.

"I never saw any other man eat as he did. I have had pretty good practice in my life; but my student friend beat both me and all my acquaintances, living or dead. 'The alderman in chains,' as they then used to denominate the turkey and sausages, had very nearly disappeared. I should have sent it away with only a modest slice cut out of its breast; but the student would not agree to that, and sliced and cut it nearly to a skeleton. I never saw, either, a better carver. Wings and legs, breast, back, and side bones, came away like magic. The student did everything with a grace; and even the landlord, who fell back aghast when he came in with

66

the second course, an immense *pièce de résistance* in the shape of a sirloin of beef, although he looked with a profoundly sad and regretful eye at the remains of the turkey, treated the student with marked respect, and placed the beef before him.

"'Landlord,' said he, 'what have you to drink? Something, I hope, that will give me a better appetite; we have been playing at present.'

"'Some hock, or some sparkling moselle?' returned our host.

"'Pish!' said the other: 'give me something fresh and new. We understand all those things. Let our friend drink light wines, and bring me some gin and bitters. Mind, the best of both, and just give the fire a poke, its spirits are gone out.'

"I was aghast! Here was one on whom I had previously looked with respect, asking for the most vulgar of vulgar liquids. The landlord merely bowed his assent, and as it was Christmas Day, I bade my guest drink what he chose to call for. He took me at my word, repeated his order to the landlord, and tossed off the bumper of gin and bitters, in a way which made me fancy that the liquid hissed as it rolled over his hot tongue. 'Ah!' thought I, ' it's a wild life they lead at college. This young man will be a ruined man.'

"I cannot say that the liquid appeared to affect him at all. He said it was water, and threw a portion of it in the fire, which blazed up in a pale blue flame, testifying to the goodness of our host's spirit, and at the same time lighting up the pale countenance of my guest, and making me mark more than ever the deep lines in his face, extending from his nose to his chin, and those which spread out from the corners of his eyes, like the lines in a map which show you which way a certain route runs.

"The beef went pretty nearly as quickly as the turkey had gone. I call my memory to witness that it was not eaten by me. I cannot remember that even without dread, nor the face of the landlord, bathed almost in tears, as he carried away just a slight shade of the sirloin. The excellent man bore in the pudding, with despair; but the landlord's daughter, who had an artistic eye, had marked a cross in honour of the day in red berries upon one side of it. It was a huge pudding, and looked nobly with the leaves crackling and glistening in the light above it.

"The pudding was carried to me. I preserved the pretty cross, not only in obedience to my own tastes, but also to that of my companion, who, when he saw it, would not touch the pudding. He took a mince-pie, and talked some nonsense about the holly-berries poisoning the pudding; but I did not heed him—I was only glad that we should redeem our character a little. I'll be bound that down in the kitchen they had called a council to consider our enormous appetites.

"The pudding, with its red cross of beads, was therefore sent away untouched except by me. The cloth removed, we turned to the fire, and the stranger, remarking that *he* 'ought to know something about fires, since he lit his own and *that* never went out,' gave ours a poke which made it brilliant in a minute. The landlord then brought in a bowl of punch, emptied a glass of it in wishing us a merry Christmas, and then hurried out of the room to his Christmas dinner. Poor man! my heart misgave me when he left; and I thought how his wife pitched into him about his guests. But if my heart misgave about the landlord, I confess it did much more so about myself. What was I to do with my strange guest. Here was he, glowering over the punch-bowl, drinking like a madman, and yet without the slightest effect being produced upon him.

"I took two or three glasses of punch just to give myself Dutch courage, and then boldly faced my guest, and asked him to give me a song. This he did not seem inclined to do, but he said he would tell me a story; and of all the miserable, wretched abominations perpetrated at Christmas time, his was the worst; I declare it gives me even now the horrors to think of it. It was a German legend about love, and ending in suicide. The love was none of your true-hearted, legitimate English love, but puny, miserable love; a love which will not fix upon a maiden object, but perversely chooser a married woman—and then, with a heart stuffed full of immorality, a brain of sophisms, and a mouth full of lies, drives the hero (?)—a pretty hero indeed!—to poison his mistress, and then to cut his own throat. I declare I felt my gall rising; I cleared my throat to speak, and trounced my guest soundly. He laughed hollowly enough, and talked about the English being excessively tame and silly, and wondered why we did not show the same spirit as our neighbours did! Heaven preserve me from such Christmas talk!

"I had made up my mind to give him a piece of it, when he opened his mouth again, and proposed snapdragon; the punch was gone, and while I played at snapdragon, he said he would brew some punch. I was terribly weary. I wished heartily that he would 'go to Quad,' as he called his dreary chamber in the old college; but I could not drive away my guest. He lighted the snapdragon, therefore, and he tucked up his coat cuffs—I declare that he wore no shirt—and showed his long, thin, bony hands at work in the brewing. He next, to give more effect to the snap-dragon, blew out the candles!

"How deadly pale he looked by the dancing fires of the spir-its! How hollowly he laughed, when I, unable to keep my eyes from him, burned my fingers in trying to grope for some raisins. Why should we two grown-up people play at such a game? Why should the flame gradually creep up my sleeves, envelope my arms, and dance about my body? Why should his shining temples glitter like silver in a cold moonlight, and of a sudden sprout with little horns of flame? Horns of flame on his temples, tufts and sprouts of flame all over his body, crawling in a quick yet stealthy manner, lighting up his ghastly cheeks, his perfectly handsome and marble face, blue on his temples, blue from his eyes, and blue from his ears; but sulphur colour, tending to a rosy flame, breaking from his mouth! I was determined to stop it, I shouted,—'Save yourself! stop it! Fire, fire!'

"Loudly as I tried to cry I did not hear my own voice, but I rolled myself on the hearth-rug in an agony of fear, and put out my own flames. When I arose, I still tried to cry; 'I know what it is,' I gasped; 'it's—I see it all—it's—spon—taneous—combus-tion!'

"'It is no such thing, Mr. Boodle,' said the strange student quietly; "'tis a little natural magic—that's all!'

"'Oh, that's all! is it, eh?' I gasped, my voice again coming to my aid; 'give me some punch, do anything to—to—'

"'To take away the fright, my dear Boodle: how absurd of you, to be sure; here—here is some punch of my own brewing.'

"I drank it rapidly. I believed then, and I believe to this day, that it was a glass of fire, hot, of course, and yet sweet, exhilarating, delicious! it ran tingling through my chest, round about my heart, through my shoulders, under my arms, making my elbows feel funny, and my very fingers as if they did not belong to me. Running downward, it made my knees knock together with a delicious *delirium tremens*, darted into the soles of my boots, warming the calves of my legs in its backward transit, and then shooting up my spine, till it settled itself in the back of my cranium and drove me mad. That was the effect of that punch—I was mad, raving mad!

"The place itself whirled round with me, and seemed motive and alive. The student sat opposite, with his elbows on the table, his ghastly face, exaggerated in its horrible whiteness, in his long claw-like hands. He gazed upon me with a face full of malice. I still drank on. Drink? I could not help drinking! the very glasses were alive. Some of them had legs, and staggered towards me with a drunken gravity, and bowed with a mock, splay-footed humility, begging me to empty them; others, not content with this, flew round my head like the brass balls of a street conjuror, whilst I, catching them with a wondrous dexterity, emptied each in its turn. Meantime, a little dog, which was basking on the mat before us, lost form, became serpentine, and burst out into a strange compound of fiendish hands, fowl-like legs, lizard tail, which, headless and monstrous, held up in its hands a tall glass of punch, and begged me to drink!

"Suddenly the clocks of the various churches struck twelve, and I was sobered in an instant; the dog, I am bound to say, became a dog again; and the glasses—but they were empty, stayed quietly on the table, and did not offer themselves to my grasp. I rocked to and fro in my chair. I did not know what to do or think—my head still ached ready to split.

"'That bill is due tomorrow,' said the student, whose face did not look so very fiendish. 'If you go on drinking like that, Mr. Boodle, you will never be able to present it. My college punch was good, was it not?'

"'Good!' cried I, bitterly; 'good!—oh yes!' then with a desperate resolution I cried, 'I'll go now, I'll go at once.' I said this because I knew it was the only to get rid of my tormentor.

"'I'll go with you,' he answered. 'You will find someone up when we get there who will give us a bed; come along—another glass, and ring the bell.'

I rang the bell. The sleepy ostler declared gruffly that 'it was a rum go, to have a hoss put to at that time o' night, and Christmas night too;' but the boots, who was not sorry to get rid of us, offered to help him, and thus the matter was concluded.

"When I got into the gig, I wrapped myself up warmly; my tormentor mounted beside me. *He* said he went to take care of me. Take care of me, indeed! We drove out into the quaint streets of the old city, with its colleges with spires and Gothic archways, the old gable ends of houses showing sharp and clear in the moonlight. No one was abroad—we drove, as it were, through a city of the dead. The moon was on the off side of us, a little to our back, so that it threw the shadow of the horse and gig, and the driver, plainly enough before us on the near side. I say the driver only, for the thing which sat by me in a ragged college gown and square cap had no shadow.

"I was not surprised. I had been horrified to my utmost. I could wonder no more. I drove forward into the open country, where the road glistened white in the moonlight, and the long shadows of the trees were thrown across our path. Out and away, far away. The mare travelled like lightning. I had a strong arm, but it ached with my attempt to hold her in.

"The road soon changed. It was no longer an English country road, but a plain straight viaduct, with water on each side of it. Multitudes of people were passing, and some strange vehicles, drawn by long-tailed Flemish horses, with plumes of feathers on their heads. The drivers were the thinnest men I ever saw, mere lanterns of men, with positively nothing in them. I struck one of them with my whip, and he sounded like a dried bladder. You might as well have whipped an empty cape. My strange friend bade me not whip those drivers, for they would one day drive me, and that men often thought them their friends. I shuddered as he said it. I saw the strange silent eagerness of the passers-by, the thousands thronging to the same goal, the ceaseless hurry of the feet, the careless look of all who trod the way, and I thought to myself that I knew what that way was.

"My companion was himself changed. He was no longer gloomy, but genial. He told me not to be in any hurry, for, said he, we were sure to get to the end of the journey at the appointed time; no one was ever known to be behind-hand, however slowly he travelled; and as for those who hurried, they were only laughed at for their pains when they arrived. Under these circumstances, therefore, I again tried to pull in my mare, upon whom the pace was beginning to tell. As we went forwards on that straight road, I saw that the poor mare grew old and out of condition, my spick-and-span new harness was cracked and appeared to be mended with ropes, and the very vehicle in which we sat, instead of being of the newest fashion, seemed worn and pelted, rotten and worm-eaten. I wondered how it could hold together.

"Some of the people whom I saw walking along the road soon grew tired of the monotony of the scene. Others declared there were no places to stay at, and indeed they were pretty well driven mad by fellows with whips, who kept urging them forward, whether they would or not. But there were some, although I confess not the majority, who were delighted with the road, and to whom it certainly did offer pleasures and advantages, for they, passing over the streams on each side of the pathway, strolled into pleasant meadows, where they lay down and disported themselves, free from evil or anxiety.

"The common passengers on the road fixed their eyes on these gay fellows, and praised their happiness, and contrasted their lot with their own; but I observed that, although they grew morose and sad at their hard condition, and the contrast thus afforded them, they seldom took occasion to observe how many were, like themselves, toiling on a painful, weary, hard road, with very indifferent clothing against the weather, and with few or no shoes to speak of. Some were so pricked and urged by the contrast, that they, taking the advice of certain evil companions marvellously like my student, who trudged by their side, threw themselves at once into the river with a despairing yell.

"I found afterwards, however, that this haste did them no possible good, for my companion told me with a malicious grin, that the river ran a great deal faster than the road, and that when we got to the great terminus we should find that these desperate people had arrived before us, sadly wetted, tumbled and bruised, and heartily ashamed of their precipitancy and haste. There were also—but they were so few that I need scarcely mention them—others who went quietly along, picking out the clean and smooth places in the road, taking no heed of much gold and silver which was strewn about, but always in foul and muddy spots; would bind up their feet as well as they could, shielding themselves and their neighbours from all harm; and who, having paced along pleasantly, we found had arrived quite freshly and blithely at their journey's end.

"I observed that a great many people who stooped down to the muddy holes, and loaded their pockets, heads, breasts, and backs with gold and silver, generally called these people fools, asses, and idiots, and despised them heartily, and would puff along under their burden, bragging how hard it was to acquire the gold and riches that they had about them, but which I am certain were very easily picked up; indeed, the only condition for picking them up was, that whoever did so must not fear the dirt, for although many began the employment with clean hands, yet I found that when they had been some time engaged in the pursuit they grew marvellously dirty.

"Poor fellows! they were to be pitied, for when we arrived near the end of our journey, I found that all of them had to throw down their burdens, aye, and to wash themselves pretty clean too, before they were allowed to enter; so that none of these, I should fancy, who took to the occupation, which was very popular, of gold-picking, got the first place.

"As for myself, I never quite reached it, but it could not, I think, have been very far off, when my strange friend gave the reins a pull, and turned the decrepit old mare into a wayside inn.

"Such an inn! It had been a magnificent church once, but now it served for meaner purposes. The oriel window had been blocked up, galleries built along the aisles, and the arches were filled with bricks. It was miserable to look at, very miserable. I shivered as I entered it.

"The student jumped out of the gig, and called for the ostler. A miserable wan skeleton of a man came and took the old mare's head. I got down, and felt terribly stiff and old. I opened the well of the gig, where my samples and my valuables, and my bill were, and took them out. I had a great mind to run away, but I did not know my road, and wanting to go to sleep, and to rid me of my companion, I called for the chamber-maid. She came. Such a woman I never saw before, and never want to see again. She was a dried mummy of a creature, with the same discoloured face, dusty eyes, and parchment mouth which a mummy has. She tried to look pleasant, I dare say, but had only that mummy look of drawing her blue lips over her teeth, ready to split them, which all mummies have. I snatched the candle from her, and asked her which bedroom I should have, but I received no answer, and rushed forward.

"The first room I found was a double-bedded room, but not caring to search further, I took it. It was a sad mouldy old place, with cobweb curtains and hangings, and enough to give one the rheumatism to look at. Anxious about my bill, and knowing that we had but few hours to sleep, I undid my dressing-case, to see that everything was all safe. In unpacking this, I happened to uncover the looking-glass in the pocket of the cover, and looking therein, found that I myself was withered down to an old, old man, and that my clothes hung bagging and worn to shreds upon me. I was proceeding with my search, when a hand was laid upon my shoulder, and the case snatched away. With rage and fury, I, knowing it must be the student—for a horrid prescience told me who it was—sprang upon him, and shouted 'Thieves, robbers, plunderers!' with all my might. My voice was not gone, that was certain.

"'Hush! hush!' said a cheerful voice, which was that of Tom Groggins, 'hush! you are all right now, isn't he, doctor? quite right; look at his eyes, he isn't the same man!'

"The doctor peered into my face, and looked quite delighted.

"'Oh, Boodle! Boodle! how you have frightened me,' said poor Tom, with a choked voice; 'we gave you up ever so many times, that we did.'

"'Gave me up," eh! where is the bill—where's the student—where the—?'

"'Now, be quiet, Mr. Boodle,' said the doctor, 'be quiet—it's all right. The bill is paid a month ago. The truth is, you, and your college friend, whom you frightened preciously, ate too much of the turkey, beef, and pudding, on Christmas Day; you've had an attack of apoplexy, then of brain fever—and now you are well over it.'

"That was the account *they* gave of it," said Mr. Boodle, looking solemnly round, "but I ignore it. I don't believe it. I believe I was ill, very ill, and enough to make me; but I will swear to every bit of the story, to the student, the inn, and the road to it—especially the dirty people picking up heaps of gold! heaps of gold!"

A Phantom of the Du Barry

How was this story told? How should it suit joyous hearts and simple, quiet homes? How should it touch them? Well, I wot, by its truth and its quiet earnestness. It will show us the reverse of the picture of the *Grand Monarque* to that which was painted by his flatterers and courtiers. It will teach us that the "hearts of kings" are sometimes not—where the prayer-book says they are.

Vanish dim figure of Du Barry, moaning and muttering with thy thin lips upon which *crème de la rose* lingers. There is a streak of rouge yet upon those cheeks, and round thy neck a deeper crimson still. Vanish along with Cagliostro there!

★★★★★★

"Monsieur Philippe Gaubert, I congratulate you; your fortune is made."

"Well," answered a quiet, handsome young man to whom the words were addressed, "well, cousin Jacques, I am glad to hear it. How so?"

Now M. Philippe Gaubert lived in the Rue St. Honoré, and kept therein a handsome shop, as indeed he should, being the court hairdresser; and, moreover, in this sweet-smelling shop, redolent with vapours of a thousand perfumes, the presiding divinity was Antoine's wife. Elise Gaubert was, in truth, as pretty a young woman as one could well meet, nor was her beauty at all diminished by the perfect knowledge which she had of it; who, indeed, could blame her for that knowledge? Did not M. le Due de Cossé Brissac, that first-rate judge of beauty, himself praise her, as he sprinkled his laced kerchief with *esprit de la reine?* Did not *Monseigneur* the Archbishop of Soissons do the same? And were the words of at least half a dozen of captains of the Swiss guards worth nothing? I trow not. Moreover, there was one friend often consulted, always complaisant—reflective, but not severely so—who said both day and night a thousand flattering things of her; in the fresh morning, when the little laced cap sat jauntily upon her glossy curls; and at night, when powder, *pomatum*, and patches had done their work upon her. That friend was her mirror.

The person who thus addressed M. Gaubert was one Jacques Carambole, *laquais de place* of the king himself, and own cousin to the pretty Elise. Jacques was a wild, flighty fellow, who had a careless face, and not the very best of hearts under his laced coat; he was the very pink of courtiers, and, having the ear of the king, used to hold his *levées* as well as his majesty Louis XV.; indeed, he had threatened to annihilate a bishop who preached against the loose morality of the court, and was only deterred from doing so by a present. In what way he worked we shall partly see; and as for the other part, one knows that with a weak and dissolute king *inuendos* go far enough.

"My fortune made, Jacques! Well, it's a pleasant thing to hear, though I am well content as I am; but tell me how so."

Jacques looked slily at Gaubert, and then said, "Put by that wig, do, and come here," and then drew him into a *salon* behind the shop.

"Philippe," he cried, looking at him, "I saw the king this morning."

"Possibly," said Gaubert.

"*Peste!*" said the valet, "and I gave him a portrait."

"You often do that," was the retort, "often; it is your office, and worn with your gay coat."

"*Ciel!*" cried the valet, impatiently, "how dull you are. The portrait was of Elise, your wife, Madame Gaubert."

The *perruquier* drew himself up, after a sudden start, and with an effort seemed to render his face as impervious as a blanket, so that the sharp eyes of his cousin made nothing out of it. "Think of that," said that worthy, with great eagerness; "expect to be chamberlain to his majesty, or to be ennobled and retire to your lands. Your wife shall be a *marquise*; she has a clever head—who knows but that Du Barry may fade before her charms, and she reign absolute, Madame la Marquise de Carambole. Speak, man!"

"Ay!" said the husband, slowly, "She takes your name?"

"Yes," answered the *laquais*; "we thought it best."

"We!" echoed Gaubert; "does *madame* know of this?"

"Know! faith, yes. She gave me the portrait, and bade me manage cleverly. Why, the Choiseuls and half the nobility would give their ears for the chance, and you—you seem interdicted—*ah, bête!*" and the *laquais*, half disgusted at Gaubert's stupidity, turned on his heel, and took a leisurely survey of himself in the mirror.

"*Bête*, in truth," muttered Gaubert, strangely. "Oh! I'm rejoiced, most happy;" and flinging aside his cousin, he opened the door and strode out of the room, with a loud, dissonant laugh.

"Well," said Master Jacques, "I never heard such hyena-like laughter. And so he's gone to give Elise the good news; *n'importe*, my hour will come," and, dipping his fair hands in a dish of rose-water, he took off his hat most politely to the *grisette* in the shop, and made his bow—as pretty a courtier as ever trod the round-stoned, inconvenient *pavé* of the time.

Philippe Gaubert went, as Jean predicted, to his wife's apartment; he was dotingly fond of her, and, as one may suppose, had spared no expense to make her happy. Elise was seated at her mirror even then, and turned round to look at him, as he entered the room *distrait* and pale; she was holding a rose to the side of her glossy curls, and with a sidelong glance marked the effect in the mirror. Gaubert looked at her seriously, long, and earnestly.

"You are such a *drôle*, Philippe," she said, beckoning with a pretty toss of her head. "Come here, sir!" Philippe' face cleared instantly; he ran and knelt at her feet.

"You love me, Elise? "he said, in a low voice.

"Of course, foolish man," she said. "How do I look?"

"Beautiful," he murmured, "beautiful as on our wedding day, but one short year ago! You would not leave me, Elise?"

"You are so dull, Philippe," pouted his pretty wife.

"Nay," said Gaubert; and he placed his large, strong hands on each side her face, drew it gently to him, and kissed her mouth.

"Should I look well at court, Philippe?"

"Anywhere, anywhere," he murmured.

"I thought so,'" she said, calmly.

Philippe started, and bit his lip; his face again assumed the stolid, marble-like expression, as he repeated, "Thought so—thought so!"

"Elise!" he said, suddenly speaking quickly—"Elise! Cousin Jacques has been here, and has shown, he says, the king your picture!"

It was her turn to start now. She ran to Philippe, and said, "You are not angry?"

Gaubert shook his head, and, without changing countenance, answered, "And so, Elise, you would be favourite of the king?"

She hesitated, looked into his passionless face, beat with her pretty foot upon the polished floor, and then said, "Yes."

Gaubert took her arm from off his shoulder roughly, and drew some paces off; his voice, however, showed but little emotion, when he said, "Why so Elise?"

"Oh, think, Philippe, think of the gaiety of the court; I wish you could have heard our cousin Jacques tell of it; of the lights and pictures; of the thousand pleasures; of admirers, courtiers, rivals, ladies—ladies who are jealous of you, who turn pale and bite their lips—who envy you and hate you." Her eyes flashed as she said this. "Think," she continued, "of one's *levées*, of one's mornings and evenings, of priests begging their living, of generals asking their command, of painters wishing and waiting, and waiting and wishing to paint one's portrait; of poets writing verses all day long to me, of handsome young officers—of a thousand things. All these, Philippe, all these, dear to us women—so dear you hardly know, you good, solid, careful old man, you—you dark-browed *philosophe!*—all these belong to the first favourite of the king!"

Heavens! had it come to this? Had the courtier's laugh and empty talk—had the subtle poison of society—had the manners of the time, aided, no doubt, by M. Jean Carambole, brought his wife to this? She evidently thought no wrong in what she said; she was bewitched; she was perverted. She had so long lost innocence of mind that to her vice had taken the place of virtue. What ho! Shuffle the cards; change places—out here, down there. Where is it?—what is honour—what was love—who was your husband—what meant the name of wife? *N'importe,* Power, place, gay dresses, and gay faces—give her those, and honour would be thrown away as worthless and unloved!

The perfumer, whose Protestant mother had taught him somewhat differently, thought that it would be worthwhile to try and rescue his wife. To rescue!—nay, to awaken her; that was all which was needed. He would try to do so,

"Think," said he—his voice sounded loudly and solemnly like a cathedral-bell—"Think, Elise, think of the ties you sever—of the sins which you commit. It is the devil's cunning, my poor girl, which gives to bad employ fine names, and sugars over vice with pretty syllables. Court favourite! I will not shock your ears with the word which common lips will change that for. Think, for my sake—for your own. Our home is dull, perhaps: this perpetual scent—this feeble, fine-dressed smell has poisoned your life and soul; for poisons live in flowers. Think of the loss of self-respect—of name, of honour; think of children, who, grown up to man's estate, dare not give the lie to the veriest wretch in France who dared to spit out venom against their mother.

"Think of days of calm happiness for ever gone; of peace wrecked, of all friends gone too; of myself a stranger; of Heaven a greater stranger still; of shoals of smiling hypocrites around you; of the path you would tread, like a journey over unsafe ice which cracks beneath your tread. Think of all these, Elise! If you do not think of the sin you commit against your husband, against Heaven, against God, oh think, at least, of the folly and the crime you perpetrate against yourself!"

His lips were parted, his cheek pale; his heart beat strongly and fast; his knees knocked with emotion; his hands were joined together as if he prayed. But, unfortunately, the word used by Philippe Gaubert grated upon the ears of his wife. Think! why she hated the very sound of those letters! Her husband was always thinking; although one of the very gayest of Parisian trades—although money came so quickly in—still he grew more and more pensive, and had hinted to her that the result of these cogitations was that he was about to leave Paris!

To leave Paris! Those words seemed like a death-knell to the frivolous beauty. Paris, to her, comprehended all that was beautiful, all that was gay in life; she could not bear the thought, and so she determined to take counsel with her cousin, who she imagined had great influence with her husband, as by his influence he attracted a great many customers to his perfumery. This, however, extended no further than the shop; and to all Jacques's remonstrances, to all his arguments, both addressed to his person and his pocket, Gaubert, who, wonderful to relate of a Parisian, absolutely had a very moderate love of gold, turned a deaf ear. .

The confidence which Madame Gaubert reposed in Jacques increased with a community of feeling. Upon Parisian life—upon its gaiety, its perpetual round of enjoyments and its elegancies, the two conversed, earnestly and often. One day Elise sought her cousin, whom she found in the very gayest of humours (he was always gay, but on this occasion especially so), singing part of a song which he had caught up from the company of comedians then playing in the "Palais Royal:"—

Buvons, chers amis, buvons!
Le temps qui fuit nous y convoie;
Profitons de la vie
Autant que nous pouvons!
Quand on a passé l'onde noire,
Adieu le bon vin, nos amours!

"*Chère cousine*," he added, tenderly, "you look sad,—a fashion of face which does not become you."

"No, indeed," answered Elise, pettishly,—"no; and yet it will soon be the only one that I shall wear."

"How so?" said Jacques.

"My husband," said Elise, with spiteful compression of her pretty lips,—"he still 'thinks' of leaving Paris."

"And of taking you with him?"

"Of course."

"Ah!" said Jacques with a nonchalant air. "A great pity that man has that very uncourtly disease of being fond, too fond of his wife."

The expression struck Madame Gaubert. She had often felt exactly what Jacques expressed, but had never dared to utter her thoughts to herself. Now, however, she was strengthened by her cousin's concurrence, and she said affirmatively, "He *is* too fond of me."

Jacques saw his advantage. He knew very well that when once a woman tires of the attentions of her husband, his affection in her heart can soon be supplanted. He acted upon the 'move' that he had gained, and played his game accordingly. He drew pictures of gallantry and gaiety at court, which at first startled, but soon pleased, the light-headed and light-hearted creature whom he had to deal with. It is useless following him step by step in his scheme; suffice it to say, that, before Elise left her cousin, Jacques had won her to consent to sit for her portrait to Greuze, and had even obscurely hinted of his purpose of presenting that portrait to the king himself.

Jacques felt that he had done enough for one day's work, and hastened to break up the interview, promising Madame Gaubert that, if everything succeeded, not only a Parisian life, but the very acme of that should be hers. Elise felt her cheeks burn as she hastened away to her husband's home; she felt, indeed, morally guilty, but the prospect before her dazzled and confused her.

From day to day the plot of M. Jacques went on, and prospered bravely. There could not be a doubt as to what would be the end, and the *laquais de place* was perfectly triumphant. Everything was as yet kept from the unconscious M. Gaubert; Jacques thought to hook his fish thoroughly before he went further, so that by the time that Gaubert was informed of the little plan arranged to make his fortune, Elise had ripened slowly and certainly, and was as ready to perform her part of the play as her excellent cousin Jacques Carambole himself.

Having paid what was perhaps due to the reader, the foregoing explanation, we will return to the *perruquier* and his wife.

"Think, Elise!" he reiterated.

"Philippe," said his wife, turning away her head from his ardent gaze, "I have thought, day and night—I have waked to think upon it—and I have dreamt of it in my dreams."

Gaubert started as if stung. "Thought!" he ejaculated—"cold-blooded, devilish calculation! My God! how could this woman sink so suddenly, so deeply as this. I cannot—will not believe it. Elise," he said again, "this is a fearful dream,—you know not what shame you seek."

Alas! the answers of Elise, full of the sophistries of Jacques Carambole, illustrated with the cases of Pompadour and Madame du Barri, too truly showed that she did indeed know the step which she contemplated. The pure-minded and thoughtful man found that, by some devilish agency, his wife's mind had grown corrupt by the side of his own; that, whilst he from thought to thought had grown better, nobler, and more pure, she had sunk downwards, step by step, from frivolity to corruption.

Gaubert groaned, and buried his face in his hands, and then said, hoarsely, "I consent—tonight, Elise, I will bid Jacques to supper, and—and—arrange all—"

To rush from his wife's room upstairs to a garret which contained but some few retorts, a little furnace, and a worm, with which he made experiments in perfumes, was for the unhappy husband the action of a moment; to beat his hands against his head, to rave, to do all else but weep, his next. He almost tore himself in his agony. "Fool! fool!" he muttered; "to marry this light girl, this spring flower, which yields but poison!" As he said the words, his eye fell upon the retort, "Poison from flowers," he muttered, "poison! 'tis just—oh, Heavens, witness that 'tis just! I'll slay her ere she be polluted; Heaven help me, but I will!"

He grew calmer in a moment, and went out into the street; so calm, indeed, that when he reached a little dingy-looking shop at the corner of the Rue du Temple—a place fashionable at one time, but decaying even then—his face had grown quite calm and stolid. He entered the shop, and was confronted by a little wiry Italian, in whose hands he placed a *louis d'or*, saying, "*Aqua Tofana, signor.*"

The man looked up into the face uncovered by a mask, a sight unusual for him, and said, "Five of these, *signor*, if you are a courtier."

Gaubert placed the money in his hands.

"Of what strength?" said the Italian.

"Let them die in an hour!" hoarsely uttered the *perruquier*.

"Good," answered the Italian, placing a small phial of coloured liquid in his customer's hands. "You are in a hurry, *signor*."

The *perruquier* made no reply, but strode forth towards his home.

In the same *salon* where Jacques Carambole had first enlightened M. Gaubert as to the honour he intended him, the three principal persons of our tale had been seated for very nearly an hour at the supper-table. It was gaily spread—very gaily—and Jacques had done most excellent justice to it; never had his spirits been higher; and glass after glass of wine crowned the feast. Elise was there, looking her very prettiest, and her eyes sparkling with unusual brilliancy. Strange to say, her husband had been more joyous than usual also, and M. Jacques thus congratulated him—

"Well, *mon cousin*, I really must own that we had our doubts of you; we thought that we should have to endure unheard-of difficulties in getting over your strange scruples—scruples which, pardon me, do not at all accord with the spirit of the age; and to live behind the age, one knows, is essentially vulgar. What says

Rochefoucauld? *Peste!* that fellow says his good things so naturally, that we either quote them as our own or forget them—however, I know he has some excellent maxim upon it."

"Moral, of course," said Gaubert, taking out a watch set with jewels, and looking anxiously at the hands.

"Of course," minced Jacques, "moral—I think Rochefoucauld intensely moral; he is always preaching to one the morality of life. Now no one is so wretchedly stupid as to fancy that M. de Soissons, because he is an archbishop, should be a follower of apostolic simplicity; but everybody expects him externally to live up to his profession, that is, to live sumptuously, and to bear himself as proudly, as an archbishop should."

"An easy morality," said Gaubert, still following the slow motion of the minute-hand.

"Why the truth is," said Jacques, "we live in an easy age. What is moral in one age is not so in another; in fact, far otherwise. But a truce to my sermonizing. I must say you have borne your honour like a—a—courtier."

Gaubert did not answer.

"Yes," reiterated Jacques, "like a courtier. That *salmi* was delicious;—but what a strange pain I have here; can it be the wine? Yes, and as you retired decently, and left it entirely to myself and Elise to settle, I must say that you have not only acted like a courtier, but also like a philosopher. Here, let us drink health and long life to *la Marquise!*"

The words had hardly fallen from the lips of the *laquais de place*, when Gaubert started up, his whole frame expanding with ire, his eyes glaring, his lips foaming and protruding: the minute-hand of his watch had touched the hour, and had rested. His time was at last come. He dashed the glass from the *laquais's* hand, and shouted,—

"So you two settled this between you, and now you wish her long life in her sin. Long life! Liar! pander! neither you nor she have half a minute to live! Long—"

Both sprung to their feet, their eyes glaring upon him—it was but for a moment, for the poison of Exili was faithful in its work. The *Aqua Tofana* touched their hearts, and they all sank into their seats, their glassy eyes fixed in a glare of hatred and astonishment, till they became stony and cold in death!

A Party With a Vengeance

I do not pretend to decide whether the old chroniclers, like Fairfax, "believed the magic wonders which they sang," but it is certain that if they did not, they told lies as enormous as any on record. This legend is related *au sérieux* by more than one respectable authority. As a reputation for learning has helped a few authors, including Sir Lytton Bulwer, I may as well give my authorities and take the benefit of the act.—*Delrio. Disq.* Mag. 1. 3, part I., and *Heyw. Hierarch.* 1. 9, p. 600.

CHAPTER 1

The Count Demánoff was as pretty a specimen of uncontrolled humanity as could well be found in the year 1557. When I say that, I have said much; but it would not be an easy task to exhaust yourself over my hero.

He was at once the pride and terror of the country in which he lived; and that country was Silesia, a province more often spoken of than visited, peculiarly adapted for the province of the novelist, and whose distance does, in more senses than one, lend enchantment to the view. Silesia is celebrated for those wonderful cascades seen in exhibitions, for those "rocky glens" and "mountain passes" produced from the brains and sketch-books of wandering artists, and prepared in the top rooms of small houses, or under the north lights of Howland-street, Fitzroy-square,—scenes which do the greatest credit to the imaginative faculties of the painters.

Silesia also produces those excellent peasants, whose faint images yet linger on the stage—peasants whose hearts overflow with habitual loyalty, and whose feelings are as fine as their complexions. The honest fellows would, at the time we write of, work like slaves, and were only too glad to pour all their little treasures at the feet of their master. They used to throng to his *fêtes*, praise his archery, smile and slap each other on the back when Demánoff made a joke, poke each other in the ribs when he kissed any of their daughters, and submit to his brutalities with a good-natured subservience, which, it is a thousand pities, seems nearly to have died out; unless it may be said to exist amongst those loyal hearts, the lower parts of whose accompanying bodies are clothed, like the stage peasants, in plush.

The unsophisticated souls in Silesia used to admire Demánoff thoroughly. *They* were never sufficiently mean to question his rights and prerogatives. They thought his every action was just, and that all his performances were the best of the sort. Thus, when Demánoff buzzed out a hunting-song, which he did most miserably, much about as sweetly as a crow imitating a nightingale, they would waggle their loyal heads, and declare the horrid sound to be delightful; when he put them out in the choruses they used continually to join in, sitting at small deal tables, outside their ornamental houses, and pouring weak liquids down their melodious throats from small tin mugs—Silesia abounds in that useful mineral,—they never said a word, but looked delightedly at each other.

They were born, honest creatures! to admire, not to envy or criticise. Nay, when the count, who was always much better dressed than any of them,—as, to be sure, a count should be, or what use is he?—when the count, I say, quaffed to them—he was always quaffing out of an immense silver cup, filled from an enormous golden tankard, which was borne by a fat-legged page (in pink silk stockings)—they all bowed graciously, and never once wanted to change *his* gold for *their* tin; nay, as proper subjects they let him spend his own gold, and take as much of their tin as he wanted. Happy peasants!

Again, when Demánoff assisted at an archery meeting, or

fired his Minié rifle at a bird, and shot, as was his wont, in a clownish awkward manner, these excellent creatures would run and stick the conical bullet into the body of the bird, which he had not hit, and bear it to him, singing roundelays of praise. If he went hunting, it was ever he who killed the boar, or so they affected to believe; though, to tell the truth, Demánoff was right glad to get out of its way. The peasants used to pass all this off in such a quiet, unaffected, simple manner, that the count believed that he was quite as clever as they thought him to be, and swore roundly that he was the greatest prince in Christendom.

Swear!—he did swear. He was always swearing. Even the priests and clergymen of his countdom admitted that he used hasty language, and were accustomed to rate the peasantry if they ever imitated the prince; but these same gentlemen, who were not behind the peasants in flattery, tried to persuade themselves that it was a manly indulgence, which the count could not well do without.

The principal expletive indulged in by the prince was one so well known to Englishmen, that foreign detractors have declared it to be a naturalized idiom of our tongue, just as the Frenchman's "*Bon jour,*" or the Hindoo's "*Salaam, sahib;*" but from the fact that it is but seldom used by ladies, by gentlemen of the clerical profession, and by the more serious persons of any religious persuasion, I am strongly inclined to think that they are mistaken. I might also urge that I myself am an Englishman, and being such, might be supposed to know a little on the subject; but I fear that the latter fact would be treated as of minor importance, and at once overruled.

Certain it is, that, be it how it may, few natives ever surpassed the Count Demánoff in the use of that expletive, which, not to deal in riddles, we take to signify, to "condemn." Some scrupulous people have held it to have a minor signification, and an altered spelling, and they urge that the true meaning of the word is to close, stop, or bung up, in which we will, for the sake of the count, follow them.

As a useful lesson for those who imitate the great man who is the hero of the story, in his eccentric propensities, a lesson which the whole of this story inculcates, we may as well chronicle one day's performances of the count.

He rose at six, having previously gone to bed at nine; for in those days laziness was not so general, or perhaps candles were not so cheap. His first action was to yawn; his next to declare that (bung it!) it was uncommonly late. He would then jump hastily from the bed, and roar out to his page Leopold to (bung him!) bring him his (bung'd) shaving-water. During the delicate operation of shaving, the (bung'd) razor would very likely (bung it!) cut his (bung) chin; although it was so (bung'd) blunt. What did the people (bung them!) sell him such razors for (bung), eh—he should like to (bung) know. Bung him if he would not—

In putting on his garments, the count still used his expletives:— "Oh (bung it!) madam," he would cry, "this won't do, you know. There's not a (bung'd) button on my (bunged) shirt; and the laundress (bung her!) has (bung it!) starched the collar so stiff, that (bung it!) it has cut my ear off." At this point he would turn nearly purple with rage, and go off (bung, bung, bung it!) with so many explosions, that his countess would turn pale with fright, and say I do not know how many extra ayes for her lord.

At breakfast the count would find (Oh, bung it!) the tea a bung'd deal too hot; or the eggs (bung them!) boiled as hard as rocks; or his haddock would be (bung it!) as salt as Lot's wife after her decease. He would read the paper of the day, and, as his wont was, blow the editor (bung his impudence!) to the very antipodes. He would want to know why that pestilent fellow (bung him !) Martin Luther could not hold his (bunged) tongue; or why the peasants (bung 'em all !) couldn't starve quietly. He would also bung his vestry, bung his butcher, bung everybody about him, and finally put on his hat, stick his hands into his green velvet *jaquet de matin*, laced with gold, and saunter into his castle-yard to look after his grooms, ask how his mare (bung her!) passed the night, and call his retainers a set of idle, lazy rascals (bung them all!).

After this he would walk through his estates, and look at the crops, finding that the (bung'd) fly had taken the turnips (bung 'em !), or that the wind (bung it!) had laid the corn. He would ride abroad, and then feeling, about the usual time (bung it !), as if he could eat a bung'd horse, he would go home to dinner perhaps a little earlier or it may be later, than he was expected— it did not matter which; in either case he would wish the cook to be bunged, and all the scullions (bung them!) at Jericho.

After dinner he slept a good deal, and, repeating the expletives above a hundred times between that meal and his tea, he would, having swallowed (bung it!) a hearty supper, and having smoked his pipe, go to bed. Being reminded before sleeping that Father Anastatius would certainly set him at least five hundred *aves* for a penance for swearing, he would cry out, "Why, look here (bung it!), he can't stop me, can he? Bung him! if I were to say them, I know I should bung it a hundred times in the task." His countess hereupon, being naturally pious, would comfort him; and the count, being reassured, would endeavour to mutter a prayer or two; only, bung it! he forgot the first word—and would then go to sleep.

The countess, poor woman, who bore to him that affection which somehow or another a bad man most frequently manages to excite in a good woman, loved the count to distraction. She would do anything for him; she thought him perfectly virtuous and good, only a little excitable. She bore him several children, and at last, fulfilling her mission, died in peace, leaving him with two fine daughters, and an infant in the cradle, of whom he was passionately fond.

Father Anastatius preached a funeral sermon over the countess; and the count, to do him justice, felt, as he said (bung it!), uncommonly miserable. What was a man to do?—a poor miserable fellow (bung it!) left with a child like that! He had a great mind to marry again; and in the meantime he took to another partner, namely, the bottle, in whose company, and that of Father Anastatius, who gave him many pious exhortations over it, he passed the time, sometimes weeping, partly through emotion and partly through wine.

CHAPTER 2

The count felt for the loss of his wife. It pains me very much to do him even that justice, because I know that choleric noblemen have from time immemorial been drawn *à la* Saracen's head, without a morsel of virtue in them; but it is certain that selfish men have hearts, and feel losses deeply enough; and also that a hot-tempered individual may be allowed to have the luxury of an affection, without doing thorough injustice to dame Nature—a lady who is frequently forgotten by the authorities we speak of.

His two daughters, who were the roses of Silesia, and who had numerous young barons devotedly attached to them, never filled in their father's heart the place of their mother, who, he observed piously, rolling his eyes upwards, was (bung it!) "a saint in heaven." The poor old heathen knew he should never get there himself, and would pitifully bewail his condition. He had (bung it!) contracted such bunged bad habits; he did not know how it was, he could not leave them; he was always (bung him!) a bad man; "But as for the countess, sir"—here he looked hard at the reverend Anastatius—"she was a saint in heaven!"

Let us accept, therefore, the count as we find him, and thank Providence for that curious belief which bad men have in others better than themselves. His Majesty King Nero, no doubt, loved someone early called away, whom he rewarded with a seat amongst the gods; and we too, after denying our victims peace on earth, comfort ourselves with awarding them a place in heaven; and very generous of us too,—only the award, after all, does not cost us much.

When the two young ladies had been sent to a fashionable school at Pesth, and were proceeding in attaining those accomplishments which were most fashionable in that period, to wit, knitting and crochet, velvet painting, hard pieces from Handel's *oratorios*, and the most fashionable dances—the *cellarius*, the polka, *valse à deux temps*, and the *redowa*—their amiable father, to cure his fit of melancholy, determined to give a party. His little son, the future hope of the province, was christened with great pomp. The peasantry, in new plush continuations, and with braces fastened with a bar across their chests, calico shirts, and wide-awake hats, assembled early to sing a song; and the count, who was affected (bung it!) to tears (at which passion the faithful fellows were touched immensely, and shook their heads in couples; wiping their manly eyes on the backs of their hand)—the count, I say, made a neat little speech, in which he alluded to his "dear departed saint," a "woman who was more like an angel," he said, "than a woman, who was too good for this world (bung it!) and who therefore died!"

The Silesians here wept openly, and the count continued—

"However, it would not do for a man *not* to be a man. He (bung it!) always made it a point to be a man! (cheers) whether in war, when he met the enemy (bung him!) at the head of his troop, or in peace, when he had to bear that silent sorrow which fell not only to the peasant, but to the peer."

At this acknowledgment of the very obscure and not before recognised fact, that the circumstance of a man's being a noble, does not entirely exempt him from the common lot, the Silesians cheered vociferously; and the ladies of the party whispered to their husbands that perhaps if they, the ladies, were taken away, they would not be so much mourned for.

"However, he was not an orator (cries of 'Go on—yes, you are'); he left that to others. Father Anastatius was the one to preach; let them hear him, and in the meantime a *fête* was prepared for his friends in the courtyard, and he hoped they would do justice to the good things below, whilst he received his company above."

This neat little speech was followed by plentiful cheering, and when the count retired from the window, the plush-continuated peasants joined in a triumphant chorus, hitched up their what's-his-names in the pauses of the song, and vowed that the count was the best master in the world.

The choleric nobleman retired to his ancestral hall highly pleased. His countess had been dead for six months, and out of respect for her and the laws of mourning, this feast was the first which he had given since that melancholy occasion. He waited upon the dais, sitting in his gilt chair, expecting every moment that his guests would come; but no, they did not arrive. My learned authorities do not state the cause of this absence: perhaps the railway trains were not true to their time; perhaps the guests did not like their invitation; perhaps—but I know only what the chroniclers tell me. Twelve good men and excellent noblemen stayed away from the feast; every one of them disappointed the count; and he, sitting in his desolate hall, wondered what was the matter, lost his patience and his temper, and banged every one of his friends up hill and down dale.

Father Anastatius, who had retired to finish his sermon upon the occasion of making the young Conrad Wolfgang Bertram Herntz Demánoff a son of the churchy—like all clergymen, we are sorry to say, he left the sermon to the very last moment,—now came in, and in a bland voice asked the count whether the guests had arrived.

"Arrived!" shouted the count, in a voice of thunder—"arrived! Bung 'em! not a bunged mother's son of them."

"Fie, Sir Count!" said the preacher.

"Oh, it's all very well to say fie!" cried the count; "bung it! But who's to put up with this; There is the boy"—

"Whom we are just about to christen," cried the preacher.

"Where are the godfathers—bung them!"

"*Pax vobiscum*," cried the father, scratching his beard; "what is to be done? the bishop is waiting; the chapel is ready. We must perform the ceremony, and get substitutes for the honoured noblemen, who—"

"Bung 'em, have not come! Guests, you call them! Well, if you call those guests—bung 'em! who put a fellow to all sorts of expense, who make him kill half a dozen oxen, four sheep, two wild boars, twenty geese, dozens of partridges, and loads of rabbits, bung 'em! Then look at the *entremets* which my French *chef* has been making, the wines which my butler has brought up, the—" And here the count left off the catalogue, and gave vent to such a series of expletives as frightened the preacher into silence. He concluded by saying, in the strongest manner possible, that as his friends had disappointed him, he wished that, "in their stead, a dozen devils, bung 'em! would come and eat up his feast."

After which, being reproved by the priest, the count felt considerably relieved, and went piously to church, leaving his house nearly empty, and the little Conrad Wolfgang in the chamber, sucking his innocent thumb, and never dreaming of the faith he was about to be admitted to, or the guests that his father had invited. So the infant crowed and slumbered, and so the priests sang; and he, whose terrible rage had produced that quieting effect, which some persons find to be the fit and great reward for putting themselves into a passion, listened to the soft chanting of the voices, and fancied that his lost wife might be singing, only far more sweetly, in a land better even than Silesia.

Tramp, tramp, tramp—through the black Silesian woods, along the dusty highways, and into the old courtyard—two by two, twelve guests arrived!

Their hats were black and slouched, their hair long and dark, and long single cockscomb feathers, tipped with a small portion of the brightest scarlet, hung pendant from their hats; their cloaks were black, and hung down over their steeds, falling almost to their heels, but there met by long black boots, with scarlet heels and wicked-looking spurs of bright steel. No lackeys followed them, and each cavalier, as he dismounted, laid the reins upon the neck of his black steed, which with a solemn step ranged backwards with the others in a line, and snorted fire—so the peasants swore—from nostrils wide and inflated, and lined with scarlet.

Black! they were all black, horse and man! The peasants throwing aside their loyalty and their tin cans, and spilling the weak beer, fled in dismay, as the twelve cavaliers entered, in a long single file, the old castle! No one saw their faces—they were black, so the serving-men swore. So the *chef*, whose moustache dropped in limp dismay, declared, as, with a dozen appeals to the *sacré nom* he fled likewise.

The footmen fled—the pages fled—the housemaids scuttled away; the four-and-twenty men in Lincoln green rushed headlong from the hall; the band—an amateur band from the neighbouring village—fell over each other in fright, leaving their instruments; and a miserable page, who got his foot entangled in the trombone, fell down the hall steps and dislocated his shoulder. The butler, coming into the hall with a black-jack full of spiced hippocras, let fell his burden, and fell himself headlong into the drum. Six serving-men hearing the noise, rushed into the hall, and fell over the butler, and then without daring to rise, rolled away, shaking with trepidation.

The *gouvernante* called in a loud voice for Father Anastatius, and then ran away, till she fell into a swoon on the lawn. Lastly, old Pierre, the most faithful, and, be it said with reverence, insolent of all old servants, who was amusing himself with furbishing up the silver flagons and abusing the underlings, fled away, with his mouth so wide open with fear, that he did not articulate plainly for a twelvemonth.

So the guests were left alone, with no one with them in the whole castle but the little boy Conrad, who lay still sleeping in his cradle, breathing softly, and smiling in his slumber.

The butler, who on account of his rotundity rolled faster than the others, was the first to reach the chapel, where the bishop, with his silver mitre on his head, was just about to open his eloquent discourse.

"Master!" he shouted, heedless of the reverend lord, and beside himself with fear,—"the guests! the guests! the guests!"

All the congregation arose. The count, who, as was his wont, was about to compose himself to sleep, arose, and was about to "bung" the butler, when he remembered the sacred character of the place. He, therefore, merely took his servant by his collar and shook him.

"Art in a fit, man?" he cried. "Well, if they are come they must wait. We can't leave the sermon for them. They kept us waiting: twelve pretty fellows they are. Twelve gents, they call"

"Twelve what!" shrieked the butler, with his eyes starting

from his head;—"twelve devils, my lord!"

The good bishop dropped his sermon in dismay; and crossed himself.

"The man's drunk!" roared the count, trying to shake him again, but failing to do so from excitement.

"Come, and see yourself," gasped the poor butler, just as old Pierre, with his mouth still open, and his tongue as stiff as if it were pickled, came and rolled, and grovelled in fear at the feet of his master.

"There really is something the matter," muttered the good Anastatius. "Pray, my lord bishop, come and exorcise these demented men." But a panic seized the bishop; he trembled so that his mitre fell to the ground with a terrible clatter—his feet refused to carry him, and he modestly begged the good father to take his crosier and go himself. By this time, too, several of the servants had arrived, and the *gouvernante*, who had recovered from her swoon, sat down on a hassock, wrung her hands, and fainted in the arms of the bishop.

"Woman!" shrieked the count, with an imprecation enough to stir the clapper of the chapel bells—"where is my boy? Where is the last gift of my sainted wife?" He shook his trembling fist in such a manner in the face of the prostrate female, that the bishop winced again.

"She left him," cried the butler, " in the cradle!—surrounded, no doubt, by those twelve—"

Father Anastatius adroitly dabbed the asperges in the mouth of the butler, and so ended the sentence; and then, with a look of contempt at his superior, took the crosier, filled a vase with holy water, and dragging the baron with him, marched boldly to the castle. The butler, a few peasants, and the boldest of the gentlemen in Lincoln green, followed closely at his heels.

Long before they entered the court-yard, they were prepared for what they saw. Yellings, bowlings, and shoutings met their ears. The great dining-hall echoed with the noise. Howlings like that of wolves, barkings like dogs, gruntings like boars,—whining, neighings, crowings, roarings, brayings, hissings, cacklings, and shriekings met their ears; and there, out of the tall windows of the dining-hall, might be seen the heads of the demon guests; some like wolves, some boars, calves, dogs, goats, and tigers.

"Come!" they shouted, "come! come hither, Sir Count, master of the feast today. You have bidden us; come, sit at the head of us,—do the honours of your table."

The count shook in terror,—his very marrow seemed turned to iced water in his bones—as an unnatural chorus of laughter burst from the assembled guests, now far off, now near, now echoing tram the corners of the old castle, and now bursting like a clap of thunder overhead. He fell upon his knees, catching hold of the priest's robe, who alone stood firm.

"Take all!" he gasped,—"take all I raze the castle to the ground,—but spare, oh, spare my son!"

Again another shout, and then the tallest of the guests held up in his arms an infant's robe, which he tore and gnashed between his wolfish teeth.

The count pressed his hands against his eyes to shut out the sight, and muttered, "Spare him! spare him!"

Father Anastatius, who, good soul! had loved the countess tenderly, crossed himself piously, and then, with a sudden resolution, rushed forward to the hall. The count fell forward on his face, giving himself up for lost; the peasants betook themselves some to prayer, and some to flight, as the stout monk, laying about him with the crosier, entered the hall. The babe was in his cradle, bawling, certainly, at the top of his voice, but safe and untouched. The priest snatched him away, defied the whole troop of bad spirits, and dashed away again, with the prize in safety. The count was beside himself with joy; and the demon guests set up a chorus of disappointed howls, as Anastatius bore away the child in triumph to the church.

"They will scarce follow us here," cried the good priest, out of breath, sprinkling himself, the count, and the child with holy water, "We never invited them *here*, Sir Count," he said, bitterly.

The count hung his head, and made an internal vow never to swear, or to invite such guests again.

"I have saved the child, my lord," cried the priest, plumping the infant into the lap of the fat dignitary of the Church.

"And broken off the silver head of my crosier," said his superior, with a rueful countenance.

"You shall have one of gold, blessed at the shrine of Loretto, to which I will make a pilgrimage—"

"And pay a thousand *marks* yearly to the Church for your sins," added the bishop, putting on his mitre, and looking with dignity on the offending count.

"Anything! anything!" sobbed the repentant father,—"since I have found my son."

******

And so the legend ends. Whether the demon guests rode away, swam away, or flew away, or how they went away, no one has chronicled—but go away they did. Whether they were twelve friends in twelve masks furnished for the occasion by the *costumier* of the period, or whether they were twelve *bonâ fide* fiends, such as were common in the dark ages, no one has been kind enough to tell us. For myself, I am content to leave it as I found it, knowing well that habitual evil temper and passionate indulgence will summon twelve devils to any dwelling on earth, whether it be the castle of a real count in Silesia, or that more humble castle which is the proud synonym for the home of an Englishman.

The King of the Gnomes

Rendered—Across the French Territory—From the Russian of Nicholas Gogol

(The spirits of Earth, Air, Water, and Fire, are known—dear and very young reader, who art not quite sure what a "Gnome" is—are known to us worshippers in fairyland and subjects of phantomocracy, as Gnomes of the Earth; Sylphides (hence the name of your parasol) of the Air; Undines of the Water; and Salamanders of the Fire. Vli is the name given in Little Russia to the monarch of the Gnomes—may His Majesty never get sight of me, no, nor of any of my readers—for they do say, that if the king ever "catches the speaker's eye," and fixes his own upon him,, that the man dies. So be it.)

There really doth seem to be something fatal in the profession of ghost-story-telling. I do not wish to enter into the question of a morbid organization both of brain and body, which is, after all, the true sedation of the case; but I call to my recollection the mysterious death of M. G. Lewis, that great English originator of tales of terror; his poem of the *Isle of Devils*, yet unfinished and fresh from his hands. Edgar Poe's unhappy fate is in everybody's mind; he, too, is unlucky in his biographer, who, determined to be original, has absolutely taken an enmity, which he does not try to conceal, against the subject of his biography. The fate—life and death, taken as a piece, and closed up so consistently, may be called by that grand word—the "fate" of Hofman, the best writer of German *diablerie* who ever lived, was as sad, as mysterious, as melancholy, as any writer of his kind could wish for. And lastly comes this sad life and death of Gogol, the first, if not the only, humorist of Russia, and author of certain phantom fancies not to be surpassed. Thus, of quite modern days, we have four men of genius, each of a different nation, employed upon parallel works of fiction of a peculiar kind, dying in an untimely miserable manner.

Guilty, too, some of them, if you like. If I went a-field I could cite other examples; certainly I could quote the death of Glanville, the English writer on witches—and the untimely end of Marlowe, our English creator of *Faustus*, and the *Jew of Malta*, dying in a tavern brawl by his own hand and own dagger, turned against him and driven into his brain by a stronger arm and wrist than his own. If we believe the religious slanderers of the poor scholar and playwright, he died with as much atheism and terror upon his lips as his own Faustus, whose death scene is not to be equalled, much less surpassed, in English literature. I say that there doth seem to be something fatal about the occupation which I, in this book, have taken up; but I hope that, as I do not pretend to the genius, great and massive if irregular, of these unhappy men, so I may escape their fate.

Of Gogol ("*prononcez, s'il vous plaît,*" says Louis Viardot, "*Gogle, en mouillant un peu l'l*"), of Nicolas Gogol, it behoves one to say some little; although I promise to hold the button of the reader, hurrying on to the story as short a time as possible. He was born in Little Russia about 1808; published certain novels in 1836, the edition of which of 1842 forms three volumes in *octavo*; and crowned his reputation by writing the comedy of *The Controller*, and a romance of Russian manners and mystery, called *Meuvtoîa Douchi* (the *Perished Souls*). Like many—let me say most—young men not born of the first *Tschinn* in Russia, he found little to induce him to stay in his country.

The young Russians I have seen and talked with are not even now unlike Gogol, and prefer going abroad to living under the shadow of their paternal government. So it was with our romancist; a greater portion of his works was written *à l'étranger.*

possibly the climate of the great country did not agree with him, for, returning to that holy land in the year 1851, he terminated a career upon a road of life—which had too many quagmires, too many steep hills, and in Russia by far too many turnpike- gates to bar his way, to make the journey very pleasant—by suicide.

Death by a man's own hand is a sad thing, even if in the instance of a half-wit, an idiot, or a fool. The gift of life is too plainly from the hands of God, that we should not mourn deeply when we see it thrown away; but more mournful a thousand times is the self-sacrifice of a man of genius.

It is hard to contemplate the death of young Chatterton, of Hoffman, of Gogol, without tears, certainly not without a creeping of the flesh and a spasmodic shudder. The gift of life there, *was* something. Who would not—that is, what noble soul amongst us would not—rather have the power, fire, and genius of Chatterton for a birthright, than the noblest dukedom in all broad England? And to think that it was spilt and thrown away, by one so young and so rash! With Gogol it is somewhat different; with both, perhaps. Those who drove them to the edge of the precipice, to the awful irremediable leap, should bear half the blame.

I believe Gogol to be unknown to the English reader; nor do I know anyone with an acquaintance with, or rather say a knowledge of, the Russ, sufficient to translate him. Mr. George Sala, whose *Journey due North* points him out as the person best fitted to the task of translation, confesses his inability to *render* Gogol, at present. The version before the reader is procured across the French border, in the same way in which Mr. Sala's story of *The Countess Nadieja*, commenced, but, unhappily, never concluded, in the *Train*, was put before us.

By Gogol, and in the version of M. Louis Viardot, *The Countess Nadieja* is called *The Memoirs of a Fool*, and is the record of the last glimmerings of sense, mingled with wild dashes of insanity, of an idiotic government *employé*, who finally subsides—I hope I use the word properly—into downright settled madness. As a study of a mental chaos, it is unsurpassed; but it is by iar a less entrancing story than the present, to which I leave the reader.

★★★★★★

No sooner did the college bell, which hung before the gateway of the friars' convent at Kiew, begin to ring, than groups of scholars from all parts of the town might be seen approaching. Students of grammar, of rhetoric, of philosophy, and of theology, with books and papers tucked under their arms, repaired to their several classes. Of these, the grammarians, who were the most youthful, amused themselves by jostling and pushing, and by calling each other names, to which their shrill *falsetto* voices gave full effect.

Bagged, torn, and dirty, for the most part, were these young fellows; the pockets of all were crammed with a miscellaneous collection of knuckle-bones, whistles, bits of pie-crust, and, at the proper season, with unfledged sparrows, taken from their nests, whose indiscreet chirruping during school hours not unfrequently brought their unlucky owners into close and unpleasant contact with the stick of the magister. The rhetoricians walked on with greater gravity; their dresses possibly a degree more free from dilapidations, but their faces bearing proofs of vivid rhetorical figures in the shape of black eyes and excrescent noses. These argumentators disputed with each other, and swore in well-sustained tenor voices.

Next came the philosophers and theologians, who spoke in tones an octave lower, and had nothing in their pockets but fag-ends of plugs of tobacco; they never troubled themselves to lay in a stock of provisions, finding it cheaper and more convenient to seize upon and devour whatever came in their way; and so strongly were they impregnated with the fumes of brandy and tobacco, that many a workman, while proceeding to his labours, scented them from afar, and stopped, with nose in air, like a well-trained hound, to sniff the grateful odours.

At the time the school hour approached, the public square also began to fill; and the women merchants of bread, cakes, melon-seeds, and tarts made of honey mixed with poppy-seed, lost no opportunity of seizing by their dresses those of the passers-by whose *caftans* were made of cloth or cotton.

"Here, lads, here," they shouted from all sides; "here are yer white rolls—here are yer honey-cakes; they are good—they are good, they are. By all the saints of the calendar, I made them myself." "Here," exclaimed an old woman, holding up a long and black article like a withered crab-stick—"here are your fine dried sausages."

"Don't ye buy of her," exclaimed her neighbour; "see what an ugly mug she has—what a frightful nose, what face, and such dirty hands!"

None of these alluring invitations were, however, addressed to the worthy philosophical and theological students, whose habits of tasting by handfuls were too well known. On reaching the college, the groups repaired to their several classes, which were held in long rooms, low-ceiled, and with small windows, large doors, and old black benches. A confused hubbub of various-ly-blended sounds soon became audible. The scholars repeated aloud their lessons to the teachers. Here the shrill and piercing voice of a young grammarian was raised to the diapason of a broken pane in one of the windows, and the cracked glass responded in unison.

In one corner a rhetorician, whose thick lips were worthy of a philosopher, recited his lesson in a bass voice, which distance softened into a baritone. The teachers meantime, while hearing the tasks, kept their eyes on the occupants of the benches, in the hope that something might be drawn from their pockets worthy of confiscation. If by chance the learned groups arrived rather earlier than usual, and it was known that the professors would be rather later, a battle by general consent was commenced, in which all took part—even the monitors, whose duty it was to preserve order and enforce good behaviour.

Ordinarily two of the theological students decided in what manner the combat should take place; that is to say, if each class should fight on its own account, or if all the students should divide themselves into two parties. In either case the grammarians began first; but by the time it had come to the turn of the rhetoricians, they contrived to slip away, and to perch themselves on the desks and benches to watch the fortunes of the day. Philosophy, with long black moustaches, then appeared in the field; and lastly theology, in enormous Cossack pantaloons.

The conflict generally terminated in a complete victory in favour of theology; and philosophy quietly repaired to its class, rubbing its sides, and sitting on the benches to take breath.

The professors, who in their youth had themselves often taken part in similar conflicts, saw at once by the flushed faces of their auditors that the battle had been hotly contested, and did not fail to punish the combatants by repeated applications of cane and leathern strap.

On holidays the students visited different houses in the town with puppet-shows, and sometimes themselves performed a play, the hero or heroine in all such cases being played by a theologian, nearly as tall as the church steeple, and who gave an admirable representation of Herodias or of Potiphar's wife. In payment for this they received a piece of linen, or a sack of maize, or half a roast goose, or such dainty.

All the students, whatever their classes, and whatever their mutual rivalries and hereditary antipathies, were alike void of means to procure sufficient for their appetites; they were not the less voracious on this account; and it would be difficult to say how many *galouchkis*, (dough cakes eaten with milk, butter, or honey), each of them would eat for supper. The voluntary contributions received on these occasions being naturally quite inadequate to the demand, the managers of the entertainment— namely, the philosophers and the theologians— were in the habit of sending out the grammarians and rhetoricians, with bags on their shoulders, to make a general battue in the gardens of the town; and the result was generally a plentiful supply of pumpkins.

But by far the most important event of the year to the students were the holidays which began in June, and at which season all the youths were sent home to their relations. The roads of the neighbourhood were then crowded with these poor scholars, grammarians, rhetoricians, philosophers, and theologians; those who had no homes of their own going with some of their more fortunate comrades. The philosophers and theologians endeavoured to turn their holidays to some account, by giving lessons to the sons of rich farmers, receiving from them in payment, a pair of new boots, or perhaps a *caftan* only half worn out.

The whole troop at starting, ate, drank, and slept in the fields; each of them carried a bag containing a shirt and a pair of stockings; and the theologians, being strict economists, generally took off their boots, which they slung across a stick and carried on their shoulders, more particularly if the roads were muddy, when they tucked their trousers up to the knee and boldly stalked on through all the puddles. If a village were perceived in the distance, the whole body turned out of the high road towards it, and, placing themselves in a row before the best-looking house in the place, bellowed forth a hymn in tones loud enough to split the ears of all within hearing.

The master of the house, some old Cossack labourer, after listening to them for some time with his head buried in his hands, would say to his wife, "These students are no doubt singing something very edifying; give them a bit of pork and whatever eatables we have." A basket of cakes, a bladder of lard, some rye bread, or sometimes even a fowl was then put into the scholars' bags, and they gaily resumed their journey. As they proceeded, their numbers gradually diminished, until only those remained whose homes were farthest from the town.[1]

On one occasion, during a journey of this nature, it chanced that three of the students started from the main road in search of a village, where their provision-bags, which had long been empty, might be replenished: their names were, the theologian Haliava, the philosopher Thomas Brutus, and the rhetorician Ti-

---

1. This description of the students of Kiew cannot fail to remind the reader of our own undergraduates of the days of Elizabeth and James. "Alas, poore scholar! wither wilt thou goe!" was the common complaint. Whipping and the stocks were the usual punishment of our sucking theologians, the Vagrant Acts of the time especially providing for the punishment of "vagabondes, wandring chapmen, beggars, and poore scholars."

berius Gorobetz. The theologian was a tall, broad-shouldered fellow, and of rather a singular character, one of his inveterate habits being to appropriate to himself whatever fell under his hands. He was of a gloomy disposition; when drunk, which was not unfrequently, he would hide himself in such out-of-the-way places, that it was no easy matter to find him. The philosopher, Thomas Brutus, on the contrary, who was of a more cheerful disposition, liked to lie down and smoke his pipe, and, when he had been drinking, to dance the *tropack*, (a national dance of Southern Russia), at college his share of punishment, what was there termed "full measure;" but he bore it stoically, saying, that what must be must.

As for Gorobetz, the rhetorician, he had not yet attained the honour of wearing moustaches, drinking brandy, and smoking a pipe. The short tuft of hair[2] on his head might be taken as a sign that his character had not yet had time to develop itself, although, to judge from the bumps and bruises with which he often made his appearance at class, one might draw the conclusion that in time he would become an excellent man-at-arms. His two companions frequently honoured him by pulling his tuft, as a proof of their high consideration, and employed him to run on errands. It was already late when they quitted the main road; the sun had set, but the warmth of a summer day was still felt in the calm, delicious twilight.

The theologian and the philosopher walked on in silence smoking their pipes, while Gorobetz with his stick cut away at the heads of the thistles that grew by the road-side; the road itself was narrow, and wound its way through thickets of oaks and walnut-trees that were dotted over the plain. Green hillocks, round as the cupola of a church, were scattered here and there; some fields of wheat had been passed, a sure sign that a village must be near, yet, after an hour's walk, no house was visible, and the shades of evening were now fast deepening around the pedestrians.

---

2. The Southern Russians shave all the hair from their heads, except a small tuft on the crown.

"The deuce take the place!" exclaimed at last the philosopher; "I thought we had arrived at a village."

The theologian made no reply, but, casting a glance around, replaced his pipe between his teeth; and all three again resumed their walk in silence.

"By all the saints," again broke forth Thomas, "not even a sign of a devilish habitation is to be seen!"

"Perhaps we shall find one farther on," replied the theologian, without taking his pipe from his mouth.

Meantime night had set in with a murky aspect, which gave little hope of moon or stars lending their assistance to wayfarers. The students at length found that they had lost themselves, and that they must inadvertently have wandered far from the main road. The philosopher, after groping about for some time, called out, "But what has become of the path?"

The theologian, after reflecting profoundly, replied, "It is an uncommonly dark night." The rhetorician roamed from side to side, and went on his knees to grope out the path, but without success.

Around them was nothing but an immense *steppe*, over which carriage-wheels had never passed. The wanderers made fresh efforts to proceed, but the country became wilder, and their embarrassment, which increased in proportion, was not lessened by a distant sound that strongly resembled the howling of wolves.

"What the deuce is to be done?" exclaimed the philosopher.

"What?" replied the theologian. "Why we must remain where we are, and pass the night here." So saying, he put his hand in his pocket to take out his flint and steel and relight his pipe. The philosopher, however, was, by no means inclined to consent to the proposition, he being in the habit, before he retired to rest, of eating a good-sized loaf and a corresponding quantity of lard, the absence of which on the present occasion caused an insupportable void in his stomach; he also, in spite of his cheerful disposition, felt rather afraid of wolves.

"Oh, no, Haliava, impossible," he rejoined; "go to sleep like dogs, without any supper! Let us try once more; perhaps we shall at last find some habitation; perhaps we shall still have the happiness of drinking a glass of brandy before we go to sleep."

At the word brandy the theologian smacked his lips. "True," said he; "it won't do to remain here."

They again started; and, shortly after, to their great delight, heard from afar the barking of a dog. After listening with attention to ascertain from what quarter the joyful sound proceeded, they, with renewed courage, directed their steps towards it, and, after proceeding a short distance, saw a light.

"A village! a village!" exclaimed the philosopher. He was not deceived in his conjecture; and, after a few minutes' walking, they reached a little hamlet, consisting, in fact, of only two houses, united by the same courtyard. A light was shining at one of the windows, and, on looking through the cracks of the gate, the students saw a large courtyard filled with the carts of *tchoumakis*, (travelling hawkers).

"Come along, boys," called out the philosopher; "don't stay behind. Let us in they must and shall."

All three at once began to knock at the gate, and to call out "Open! open!" The gate turned on its hinges, and the students saw before them an old woman, covered with a sheepskin cloak.

"Who is there?" she inquired in a husky voice.

"Travellers who have lost their way," was the reply. "Let us in, good woman; open fields and empty stomachs are both disagreeable things to put up with."

"And what kind of people are you?"

"Very inoffensive ones: the theologian Haliava, the philosopher Thomas, and the rhetorician Gorobetz."

"Impossible!," murmured the old woman. "Our rooms are all full, and every corner of the house is occupied: where can I put you? I know what you theologians and philosophers are; and if I were to admit such drunkards, we should be eaten up, and have all our things broken into the bargain. Get along with you; there is no room here for you."

"Take pity on us, good woman, and do not allow three Christians to perish. Put us where you like, and if we do any mischief, may our hands wither."

The old woman appeared to yield to their entreaties. "Well," said she, after a moment's reflection, "I will let you in, then; but I shall place you in three different parts of the building; for I should not feel easy if you were all together."

"Do what you please; we shall not object," replied the students.

The gate again creaked on its hinges, and they entered the courtyard.

"Well, good woman," said the philosopher, following her, "is there not a little bit of something one could have, eh? I feel as if one of those carts was driving round my inside. Since morning, I have not had a morsel of bread in my mouth."

"There! there!" exclaimed the old woman; "I knew how it would be. I have nothing for you, I tell you—nothing. I have not even had a saucepan on my fire today."

"But we would pay you honestly for all we had tomorrow," said the philosopher, adding, in an undertone, to himself, "or perhaps at some other time."

"Come on, come, and be content with what you get, my fine gentlemen," cried the old woman, impatiently. At these words the philosopher's face became woefully elongated, but as suddenly resumed a brighter aspect as the smell of dried fish saluted his nostrils. He threw a hasty glance around him, and saw, peeping from the breeches pocket of the theologian, who walked before him, an enormous tail of a dried fish, which that worthy had found time to abstract from one of the carts in the courtyard; not from any love of the fish, but from sheer force of habit; and having already forgotten his prize, and being on the lookout for another, his philosophic friend had no difficulty in transferring the fish to his own pocket.

The old woman now conducted them to their several places of rest, introducing the young rhetorician to the house, shutting up the theologian in a small shed, and assigning to the philosopher an empty sheep-pen. This last was no sooner left to himself than he devoured his dried fish; then, looking round the inclosure and kicking a pig, whose curiosity had induced him to thrust his snout through a crack, he threw himself on the ground, prepared to sleep like a top. Suddenly, however, the gate of the inclosure opened, and the old woman, crouching to the ground, entered.

"Well," said the philosopher, "and what do you want here?"

The old woman made no reply, but came towards him with open arms.

"Oh! Oh!" thought the philosopher to himself; "here's a pretty affair; but it won't do, old lady." He drew back; but the old woman still continued to advance. "Come, come, my good woman," he called out, "leave off joking; what is it you want?"

The old woman made no reply, but with outstretched arms still sought to catch him. A vague terror seized the poor philosopher, more particularly when the eyes of the old woman suddenly began to sparkle.

"Woman, in the name of heaven, what is it you want?" he exclaimed. "Begone, I say!"

Without answering, she laid hold of him with both hands. He shrunk from her grasp, and turned to fly; but the old woman had placed herself before the gate, and, fixing her glistening eyes upon him, again approached. He sought to push her back, but, to his great surprise, discovered that he had no longer strength to raise his hands or to move his legs; his very voice had lost all power, and his words were without sound; his heart alone still beat with violence.

The old woman approached, seized him, crossed his arms upon his breast, bent down his head, and with the agility of a cat, then sprang upon his shoulders, striking him with her broom and driving him onwards like a prancing horse.

All this was done so rapidly, that the poor philosopher had not even time to recover from his bewilderment. His first impulse was to seize with both hands his legs, in order to put a stop to their involuntary movements; but oh! wonder! they still persisted in bounding and frisking in a manner that might have put an Arab horse to shame. It was only when they had left the hamlet far behind, and that an immense expanse of plain, bordered on one side by a dark forest like a black line traced upon it, met his eyes, that he recovered himself sufficiently to exclaim,—"This must certainly be a *witch!*"

The rising moon spread around a faint light, scarcely sufficient to penetrate the thin veil of mist which midnight had thrown over the earth. Wood, meadow, valley, and hillock, all appeared to sleep with open eye; not a breath of wind was stirring, and the night itself felt warm and humid.

It was on such a night that the philosopher Thomas galloped, after so strange a fashion, with so strange a rider on his back. Perspiring at every pore, he experienced sensations of inexpressible, yet pleasing pain—a sort of fiendish pleasure, the deep intensity of which was terrible. At times he felt as if his very heart had ceased to beat, and, full of terror, he placed his hand on his breast; bewildered, worn out with fatigue, he then tried to recollect all the prayers he had ever learnt, to repeat all the exorcisms of which he could think.

Suddenly he felt relief; his progress became less rapid, the witch clung less tightly to him, his eyes were no longer dazzled by supernatural visions. The moon shone brightly and clearly. "This is better," thought the philosopher to himself, and he immediately began to recite aloud one of his exorcisms. In an instant, with the rapidity of lightning, the old woman slipped off his back, and as quickly did he mount on hers.

The witch at once set off at a mincing pace, which, however, became so rapid that the rider could scarcely breathe. The earth appeared to fly from under him, and the plains over which they scoured to form but one unbroken level. During this rapid flight he contrived to seize upon a stick, and with it he began to beat the witch with might and main. She gave utterance to loud shrieks, that at first were passionate and menacing; but gradually, as they became more feeble, were gentle, soft, and pleasing, until at length they sounded like the tinkling of silver bells.

Involuntarily the philosopher asked himself, "Can this be an old woman?"

"Oh, I can bear it no longer!" she exclaimed, in a voice broken with anguish and suffering, and she fell to the ground motionless. He stooped down to look at her: the day had just begun to dawn, and the gilt cupolas of the churches at Kiew were visible in the distance. To his horror and amazement, he saw extended at his feet a young and beautiful girl, with rich flowing hair in disorder, and with eyelashes long and straight as arrows. She was senseless, and had thrown her white bare arms outstretched above her head.

As he gazed, she moaned, opened her tearful eyes, and looked piteously at him. He trembled like a leaf, agitated by pity, terror, and by an indescribable emotion that at length induced him to run as if for life, his heart beating with a violence that he himself could scarcely believe credible. In this state, little disposed again to take a trip in the country, he returned to Kiew, there to ponder over his extraordinary adventure.

Nearly all the students had by this time left the town, and were dispersed in its environs, some as teachers, some as idlers; for even these found little difficulty in obtaining from the hospitable country people *galauchkis*, cheese, milk, and other dainties, without expending a farthing. The old ruin of a college was completely deserted, and not all the careful researches of the philosopher in all the comers of the place were sufficient to enable him to discover a morsel of lard or a crust of white breads such as the students were in the habit of hiding. His good fortune did not, however, desert him; for, while walking in the market-place, an old lady, a vender of ribbons, shot for fowling-pieces, and cart-wheels, with whom he was a favourite, invited him to her house, and there regaled him with delicacies innumerable.

Nor was her liberality confined to this good treatment. Some evenings after, our philosopher might have been seen at a tavern in the neighbourhood, lying at full length on a bench—his favourite posture—smoking his pipe, and with a large tin pot before him, to pay for the contents of which he had boldly thrown to the Jew tavern-keeper a piece of gold. Thus luxuriously enjoying himself, he surveyed the passers-by with a calm, indifferent air, forgetful even of the memorable night's adventure.

It was at this precise period a rumour was spread about the town, that the daughter of one of the richest *centeniers*, (a member of the military order of nobility), whose estate was at a short distance from Kiew, had returned from a walk, a few days previous, so bruised and injured from a severe beating she had received, that she was almost unable to walk; it was also said that she was now at the last extremity, and that she had expressed a wish that the prayers for the departing soul, which it was customary to repeat three days after death, should be read by one of the college students named Thomas Brutus. The philosopher learnt this from the rector himself, who sent for him, and informed him that he must start without delay, as the lady's father had sent his men with horses and a *kibitka* for him.

The philosopher trembled without knowing why, a kind of presentiment whispering that something terrible would happen to him. He therefore, without hesitation, declared that he would not go.

"Indeed!" replied the rector, who sometimes condescended to speak civilly to his subordinates; "now listen to me, friend. No one thought of asking you whether you would like to go or not. I will merely remark that, if you do not, you shall be so well flogged that you will feel little inclination to go anywhere afterwards."

The philosopher walked away, scratching his ear, and without uttering a word; but he determined, nevertheless, to take to his heels as soon as opportunity offered.

He was descending, in rather a pensive mood, the staircase which led into the courtyard, when he heard the rector saying to someone—

"Thank your master for the eggs and for the heron, and tell him that I will send him the books of which he speaks in his letter as soon as they are ready; I have already given them to a writer to copy. And don't forget, my friend, to say to your master from me, that I am told he has excellent fish in his ponds, particularly sturgeon: I hope he will send me some, for fish at our market are both dear and bad. Here, Iavtoukh, give these good people a glass of brandy each; and, my good friends, look after the student Thomas, or else he will soon give you the slip."

"Only think of that wicked old rascal putting them on their guard," muttered the philosopher, who had listened attentively to the rector's address.

On reaching the courtyard he saw a *kibitka*, which at first sight might have been taken for a barn on wheels, so long and deep was it; it was, in fact, one of those vehicles common to Cracovia, in which the Jews, with their loads of merchandize, travel from town to town whenever a fair is held. Six stout, rough-looking Cossacks were in attendance, their *caftans* of fine cloth, ornamented with tags, giving proof that they belonged to a rich and powerful master; scars on different parts of their persons might also have been shown in proof that they had not been strangers to warfare.

"Well," muttered the philosopher to himself, "it's of no use complaining—what must be must be;" and, addressing himself in a loud voice to the Cossacks, he bade them good morning.

"Good morning, sir," replied one of them. "Well! so I am to go with you; what a splendid *kibitka*," he continued, raising himself on the footboard; "we have only to engage a band of musicians, and we can have a famous dance in it."

"Yes, it is a fine carriage," replied one of the Cossacks, seating himself by the driver, whose head was enveloped in an old clout instead of his cap, which he had already found time to leave in pawn at a tavern. The other five entered the *kibitka*, and seated themselves on bags of various things which had been bought in the town.

"I am curious to know," said the philosopher, "if this *kibitka* were laden with goods, such as salt or iron, how many horses would be required to draw it?"

"A great number, certainly," replied, after a long interval, the Cossack who had seated himself by the driver, and who, having made this profound remark, considered himself entitled to maintain a profound silence during the rest of the journey.

Our philosopher was very desirous to know who the *centenier* was, what was his character, and to learn something about the daughter, whose strange adventure had been so much spoken of, and with whom he was now very strangely mixed up—in short, to acquire some information respecting the place and people to which he was going; but all his questioning was in vain—the Cossacks were probably also philosophers, for they made no reply, but continued to smoke their pipes. At last one of them, addressing the driver, said, "Take care, Overko, you lazy old rascal, that when we reach the tavern on the road to Tchoukraïloff you don't forget to stop and to awake me and the others, if we happen to be asleep." After delivering himself of this lengthy speech, he threw himself back, and speedily commenced snoring. His caution to the driver was, however, quite needless, for no sooner did the tavern come in sight than all at once roared out—

"Stop!"

This was needless. Overko's horses were so well trained that they always pulled up of their own accord, as soon as they came opposite a pot-house.

Notwithstanding the heat of a July day, they all got out of the *kibitka* and entered the dirty little tavern, where they were received with open arms by the Jew landlord, with whom they were evidently well acquainted. At their request he brought forth, holding them with the hem of his garment, several sausages, which he placed on the table, turning away his head from the forbidden meat. All were soon seated, and a large earthen jug was then placed before each guest, not forgetting the philosopher. As the southern Russians are in the habit, when drunk, of embracing each other, and of crying, it was not long before the tavern resounded with their tender salutations.

"Come, Spirid, let me embrace you."

"Let me hold you to my heart, Doroch."

One of the Cossacks, the eldest of the party, with long gray moustaches, leaning his head upon his hand, sobbed as though his heart would break, saying that he had neither father nor mother, and was alone in the world; while another, his companion, a deep thinker, endeavoured to console him by repeating, "Don't cry, I beg! don't cry—we all have our sufferings."

A third—he who was called Doroch—became excessively curious, and overwhelmed the philosopher with questions. "I should like to know what you really learn at that college; do they teach you what our priest reads in the church, or something else?"

"Don't ask him," called out the thinker, in rather a thick voice; "everything is as it is; whatever is there is there."

"No, no," repeated Doroch, "I want to know what they have in their books; perhaps something quite different from what the priest has."

"Oh," insisted the thinker, "why ask such things? whatever is is, and can't be changed, must be."

"I want to know all that is written in the books. I tell you I will know; do you think I won't find out? I will, I tell you."

"Oh dear! oh dear!" exclaimed the thinker, letting his head fall on the table, too much overcome to hold it up any longer. The other Cossacks spoke of their masters and of the reason why there should be a moon in the heavens.

The philosopher, seeing this general confusion, thought he would profit by it and escape. Addressing himself, therefore!, to the old Cossack who was crying and lamenting that he had no father and mother, he said, "See, my poor uncle, how you are crying! and I also am an orphan! let me go out; you do not want me here."

"Yes, let him go out," said some of them. "He is an orphan; let him go where he pleases."

"Ah yes!" cried the consoler, lifting up his head, "let him go, let him go;" and the Cossacks were now all desirous to take him themselves into the fields, all except Doroch, who held him back, saying, "No, no! I want to talk to him about the college." It was, moreover, doubtful whether the philosopher himself was capable of making his escape, even had there been no obstacle;

for, on rising from the table at which he sat, his feet appeared to have suddenly become incapable of motion, and he saw so many doors in the room that he would have been puzzled to discover the right one.

It was only towards night that it occurred to the travellers that it was necessary for them to continue their journey. Packing themselves as they best could in the *kibitka*, they then started off, whipping the horses, and roaring out a song of which it would have been difficult to ascertain the words or the melody. After wandering about for several hours, continually deviating from a road which they all knew by heart, they at last descended a steep hill leading to a valley, on each side of which the philosopher saw hedges, and behind them trees and the tops of houses; it was, in fact, a large village belonging to the *centenier*.

The midnight hour was already passed, and numerous twinkling little stars shone in the dark blue sky. No lights were to be seen in any of the houses, but as the *kibitka* drove into a large court-yard amid the barking of dogs, barns and thatched cottages might be perceived on each side, while at the further end of the court was a house which, from its size, appeared to be that of the *centenier*.

The travellers alighted, and entering a sort of bam, speedily betook themselves to repose. Our philosopher was desirous of examining the exterior of the abode; but, although he rubbed his eyes most vigorously, was unable to see clearly, and after several vain efforts, retired like the others to sleep. On awaking in the morning he found all the household much excited, the daughter of their lord having died during the night.

The servants hurried to and fro alarmed and bewildered —some of the old women crying, either from grief or agitation. Outside the hedge which surrounded the courtyard, a number of persons had collected from curiosity, peeping through as if there were anything to be seen.

The philosopher had now time to examine the buildings which, on the previous night, had eluded his inspection. The house itself was small and low, as it was then the custom to build in Southern Russia, the roof thatched, and in the sharp-pointed portico, which was plastered with yellow and blue flowers and red crescents, was a round window that resembled an eye with a very arched eyebrow. The portico itself was supported by small pillars of oak, the upper parts round and the lower hexagonal, and with curiously-carved capitals.

Within the porch, and on each side, was a bench; similar porches and on similar columns, except that they were twisted, were to be seen on the other sides of the house, in front of which was a large pear-tree with a top of a pyramidal shape. Several barns were built in the courtyard, and formed a sort of street which led to the principal entrance of the house; behind the barns, and near to the entrance, were two small triangular wine stores facing each other, also covered with thatch. On each of their three sides there was a small door, covered with different paintings. On one was represented a Cossack seated on a cask, and holding above his head a large pitcher, with this inscription, "I could drink all this." On another, there was a large bottle, some glasses, a pipe, a tambourine, and the inscription, "Wine is the Cossack's delight."

Through the round window of one of the outhouses might be seen a large drum and several brass trumpets, and outside the door two small mounted cannon; all these things gave proof that the master of the place was fond of enjoying himself, and that holidays were frequent there.

The country around, as seen from the courtyard, appeared so delightful—and the verdure of the meadows, through which the Dnieper, glistening in the morning sun, wound its course, appeared so refreshing—that our philosopher was enchanted, and murmured to himself, "This is the place to live in, to fish, and to shoot. One might also prepare dried fruits to sell in town, or, better still, to make brandy of them; no brandy like that prepared from fruit; and, by the bye, I might as well think about making my escape," he remarked, as he just then discovered behind a hedge a path almost hidden by long grass.

He stepped mechanically into it with the intention of sauntering on until he got to some distance from the house; and then gradually to increase his pace and escape. But this scheme was suddenly arrested by a heavy hand being laid on his shoulder, and on turning round he saw before him the old Cossack who, on the previous evening, had so deeply lamented his orphan state. "It is no use, Mr. Philosopher," he exclaimed, "to think of running away; we are not in the habit of letting anyone escape whom we wish to keep; and besides, the roads are bad for a foot-passenger. You had better come and see our master, who has been inquiring for you."

"Certainly," replied the philosopher, "with much pleasure; let us go;" and he accordingly followed the Cossack.

The *centenier*, a man advanced in years, with long gray moustaches, and with an expression of deep grief on his features, was sitting at a table in his room, his head supported by both hands; his care-worn and pallid countenance bore witness to his sufferings, and showed clearly that the gay, careless life he had hitherto led had passed away forever. On perceiving the philosopher and the Cossack, he removed one hand, and with a slight movement of his head returned the profound obeisance they made. They remained standing in a respectful attitude near the door.

"Who are you, and whence do you come, my friend?" he asked, in a voice remarkable neither for harshness nor for affability.

"I am a student—the philosopher Thomas."

"And who was your father?"

"I really don't know, sir."

"And your mother?"

"I have not the least idea: now that I consider the matter, I certainly had a mother—but who she was, or where she came from, or where she lived—I really don't know."

The *centenier* reflected for some minutes, and then said, "And how did you become acquainted with my daughter?"

"I never was acquainted with her, sir, I swear."

"Why, then, should she have chosen you so particularly to say prayers for her?"

The philosopher shrugged up his shoulders and replied,

"Impossible to say, sir; gentlefolks sometimes have strange whims, for which not even the wisest can account. What says the proverb?—'*Jump, black dog, just as your master tells you.*'"

"You are talking nonsense, sir philosopher."

"May a thunderbolt strike me if I am, sir."

"Alas!" sighed the *centenier*, "had she but lived a few minutes longer I should have known all; 'Let no one,' she said, 'let no one here, papa, read prayers for me, but send to the college at Kiew for the student Thomas; let him pray three nights for my sinful soul; he knows—' But what more she would have said I could not make out; she, poor little darling, was unable to give utterance to more words, and died. As for you, good man, you must be well known for the sanctity of your life and for your pious deeds; no doubt, my daughter must have heard of you."

"Who, I!" said the philosopher, starting back with surprise; "the sanctity of my life!" he continued, looking straight at the *centenier*, "What, in the name of goodness, can you mean, sir? Why, although it is certainly improper to say so, I actually kissed the little pastry cook last Holy Thursday!"

"Nevertheless, she must have had some good reason, for fixing upon you; you shall begin your pious offices from today."

"Well, sir, as you please: every man does the best he can, but I really think if you were to call in a deacon, or a sub-deacon even; they are learned people, and know how these things should be done. As for me, I have no voice; and then only look at me; is my appearance that of one for such a purpose?"

"All this is a matter of perfect indifference to me; what my poor girl desired to be done shall be done, and if you read prayers as she wished for three nights, you shall be well rewarded; if not, woe to those who oppose me!" These words were uttered in so very decided a tone, that the philosopher was at no loss to understand their significant meaning.

"Follow me," said the *centenier*.

They went out into the vestibule, and the *centenier* opened a door exactly opposite that of his own room. The philosopher hesitated for a moment, and then, not without a feeling of dread, entered the chamber. The floor was covered with a coarse red cloth; in one corner, near the holy images,[3] and on a high table covered with blue velvet fringed with gold, lay the dead body; large wax tapers surrounded with branches of *katina* were placed at .the head and feet, throwing out a pale and sickly light, which was lost in the brighter rays of the sun. The face of the corpse was hidden from the philosopher by the inconsolable father, who, with his back towards the door, was bending over the body and addressing it in low but emphatic tones, which were not lost upon his hearer.

"What I most regret, my dear child, is, not that you have thus abandoned me in the flower of your age and before the time allotted to you had expired, leaving me lonely and sorrowful; what I do regret, my lost one, is, that I do not know your implacable enemy, he who has caused your death. Had I but known that any one even thought of injuring you, I swear he should never again have seen those dear to him, had he been an old man like me; and that, had he been young, his body should have gone to feed the wild beasts and birds of the *steppes*: but woe to me, my flower of the fields, my bird, my life. I must pass the remainder of my days without even the shadow of a joy, compelled to wipe off with the hem of my robe the tears that will fall from my withered eyelids—while my enemy will live in enjoyment, and will in secret laugh at the helpless old man."

He ceased, exhausted, unable to give further vent to his grief than by a flood of tears. The philosopher was touched by this deep affliction, and gave a slight cough as a prelude to some remark he was about to make. The *centenier* turned round and pointed to a seat near the head of the corpse, placed before a small stand on which were several books of prayer.

"Three nights will soon pass," thought the philosopher, "and then I can go away with my pockets filled with *ducats*." He walked up to the desk, and, after having again cleared his voice, began to read without lifting his eyes from the book, determined not

3. It is customary in Russia to place consecrated images in a corner of every room.

to look upon the dead body; nor was it till the *centenier* shortly afterwards having left the room, that, slowly turning his head, he—. A convulsive trembling seized him; before him lay a form, of that rare beauty which is seldom seen on earth; she appeared alive; her forehead, white and pure as snow, seemed radiant with thought; her eyebrows, delicately fine, yet strongly marked, were gracefully curved over the closed eyes, the long lashes of which fell on cheeks still tinged with a soft hue; her lips were slightly parted, as if about to smile.

Yet amid all these charms the philosopher saw, or fancied he saw, an indescribable something, fearful and terrible. He felt such a shudder pass through his frame as might be experienced by a happy, joyous group, were someone in the midst of their frolicsome mirth suddenly to intone a death chant; it appeared to him as if his hearths blood tinged the still ruddy lips of the corpse. At once the horrible truth flashes upon him—the fatal resemblance. "The witch!"' he exclaims, in a voice choked with fright. He staggers, turns pale, and, not daring to lift his eyes, stammers forth a prayer. It was indeed the witch he had killed!

At sunset the bier was carried to the church, the philosopher supporting one corner, over which the black pall fell upon his shoulder, chilling him as though it were of ice. The *centenier* walked first, supporting also the narrow home in which rested all that he most loved. The wooden church, darkened by age and covered with green moss, with its three cupolas in the shape of cones, formed a dismal erection at one end of the village; and from its neglected state, it was easy to see that it was long since divine service had been performed there.

The open coffin was placed immediately opposite to the altar; the old father embraced the corpse for the last time, prostrated himself, and then left, giving orders that the philosopher should be taken home and well attended to, and brought back to the church after supper. All then returned to the house, and on entering the kitchen, those who had carried the bier placed their hands against the fireplace, a custom of the Southern Russians when they have seen a dead body.

Hunger, which had now begun fiercely to attack the philosopher, caused him for a time to forget all about the deceased. Meanwhile, the household began to assemble in the kitchen, which was a sort of club-room for all, even the dogs, who, wagging their tails, made their appearance at the door to receive their share of bones and scraps. Wherever a servant was sent, and whatever the errand might be, he never failed to begin by passing through the kitchen, to rest a little and smoke his pipe. All the unmarried men belonging to the establishment, who wore the Cossack *caftan*, were to be found lying down there during the day, some on benches, some under benches, some on the oven, in the fireplace, and, in a word, wherever it was possible to stretch themselves.

And then each of them forgot his cap or his whip, or something of the kind, in the kitchen, and was of course under the necessity of returning for it. The chief gathering, however, took place at supper-time, when the *tabountchik* who had then brought the horses from the *steppe*, and the herd who had taken his cows to the cow-house, as well as all the others whose occupations had kept them away during the day, were then able to join. During supper even the idlest tongues found time to wag freely; one would tell of his new pantaloons, another that he had seen a wolf, while a third, more learned, would talk of the wonderful things that were to be found in the centre of the earth. Nor was there wanting someone to say smart things—a gift not unfrequent amongst the Southern Russians.

The philosopher joined the circle that was formed before the threshold of the kitchen, whence shortly afterwards a peasant girl in a red cap came out, carrying with both hands a large smoking pot of *galouchkis*, which she placed in the midst of the hungry expectants, each of whom drew from his pocket a wooden spoon or a skewer. As soon as the first sharp cravings of appetite had been satisfied, and the rapid movement of jaws had in some degree diminished, several of the party began to talk. The dead body was of course the subject of conversation.

"Is it true," said a young shepherd, who carried fastened to his leathern shoulder-belt so many buttons and plates of copper that he appeared to be a walking brazier's shop; "is it true that our young lady was on terms of acquaintance with evil spirits?"

"Who—our young lady?" replied Doroch; "she was a witch, I tell you; I can take my oath she was a witch?"

"Hold your tongue, hold your tongue, Doroch," said a third, "that is no affair of ours. Heaven keep her! it is not for us to talk of these things."

But Doroch was not at all disposed to hold his tongue; he had just been with the butler to pay a visit to the wine-cellar on business of importance, and, after leaning a few times over some casks, had become quite lively and chatty.

"Why should I hold my tongue? "he replied. "I tell you that she made even me give her a ride, and I am ready to swear it."

"Tell me, uncle," said the young shepherd of the buttons, "is it possible to know a witch by any particular mark?"

"Impossible, quite impossible," replied Doroch, in a very decided tone; "you might read all the Psalms, one after the other, and then if you saw one would not know her."

"It is possible, it is possible, Doroch," chimed in one of the bystanders; "the learned people say that all witches have small tails."

"All old women are witches," remarked an old Cossack, very gravely.

"And you, all of you," said the girl, who had brought in a fresh supply of *galouchkis*, "are all great hogs!"

The old Cossack, whose name was Iavtoukh, grinned with delight at the success of his joke, and the shepherd burst out into a laugh so loud and deep that it sounded as if two oxen, having met nose to nose, had both begun to low at the same time. The conversation that had been carried on had roused the curiosity of the philosopher to the highest pitch; and being desirous of learning all he could respecting the deceased, he again addressed himself to his neighbour, and said, "I should like to know why all the good folks here have made up their minds that the young lady was a witch. Did she ever injure any one? Did she ever cast spells around anybody?"

"She did all that," replied one of the guests with a face as flat as a spade; "who doesn't recollect Mikita, the huntsman, or—"

"And what about Mikita, the huntsman?" said the philosopher.

"Stop, I'll tell you all about Mikita," called out Doroch.

"No, no; I'll tell him all about the huntsman," said the horse-keeper, "he was my godfather."

"I'll tell the story myself," persisted Spirid.

"Yes, yes!" they all cried out; "let Spirid tell it."

And Spirid accordingly began.

"You, mister philosopher, didn't know Mikita; ah, what a man that was! I assure you he knew every dog in the place, as if he had been the dog's father. The present huntsman, Mikola, he who sits down there, is not worthy to wipe his shoes, although he understands his business very well; but, compared to Mikita, he is nothing but dirty water."

"Very well, very well, indeed!" said Doroch, giving a nod of approbation.

Spirid continued:—

"He would see a hare in the fields before anyone else could rub his eyes. I think I see him; he had only to whistle and call out, 'Seize her, Rasbor! seize her, Bistraya!' and then he would gallop his horse at such a rate that whether he got before the dogs or the dogs before him it was really impossible to tell. And then he would toss off a glass of brandy before you could say stop! Ah, what a huntsman he was! After some time, however, he could do nothing but look at our young lady; whether he was stupidly in love with her, or whether she bewitched him, no one can say; but certainly he became a lost man, an ass, a beast— in fact," continued Spirid, spitting on the ground, "it would be improper to say what he became."

"Well—very well !" said Doroch.

"If our young mistress looked at him, the bridle would fall from his hands; he forgot the very names of the dogs, and knew not what he was about. Well, once he was in the stable, looking after his horse, when she, the young mistress, went in to him, and said, 'Mikita, let me put my little foot upon you;' and he, the fool, quite delighted, replied, 'Not only your foot, but seat yourself upon me altogether if you so wish.' She lifted up her foot, and when he saw how small and delicate it was, the charm worked still more strongly, and he became quite stupid. He bowed down his shoulders, and laying hold of her two feet with his hands, began to gallop across the fields like a horse. No one knows where they went, but he came back half dead. From that day he began visibly to fall away, and at last, when somebody went once into the stable, they found, instead of him, nothing but a handful of cinders near an empty bucket. He had burnt away to nothing—and all of himself. Ah, we shall never see such a huntsman again!"

No sooner had Spirid finished his tale, than all the company began to sing the praises of the defunct huntsman.

"*A propos*, do you know the story of the Cheptchikha?" said Doroch, addressing the philosopher.

"No, indeed."

"Ah hah! I see they don't teach you much, after all, at your college. Well, then, listen. We have here in our village a Cossack named *Cheptoun*, (meaning "the whisperer"). He is a very good fellow, rather fond of stealing and lying at times, but still he is a good Cossack. He lives near here. Well, one day, at about this hour, Cheptoun and his wife after having supped, prepared quietly to go to sleep, and as the weather was fine Cheptchikha, (feminine of *Cheptoun*), went to bed in the courtyard, and Cheptoun in the house. No, no; Cheptchikha in the house, upon a bench, and Cheptoun in the courtyard."

"You are wrong," interrupted an old woman, who was standing near the door with an elbow in one hand and her head in the other; "you are wrong; Cheptchikha didn't sleep on a bench, but on the floor."

Doroch looked at her, then looked on the ground, again looked at her, and, after a moment's silence, said,—

"If I were to tie your coats above your head, it would be

rather unpleasant, wouldn't it?"

This hint proved sufficient, and the old woman gave no further interruption. Doroch continued:—

"In a cradle which hung in the middle of the room was a child about a year old; whether it was a boy or a girl I really don't know, but that's no matter. Well, the Cheptchika had laid herself down, when she heard a dog scratching at the door, and howling in a manner to alarm all the wolves in the neighbourhood. She of course was frightened, for women are so stupid that, at night-time, if you only go behind a door and loll your tongue out at them their souls sink into their shoes. However, she thought to herself, 'I must muzzle that dog, and try to stop his howling;' so she got up, and went to open the door, but had scarcely time to do so when the dog sprang by her into the room, and went straight to the cradle.

"The Cheptchikha then saw that it was no longer a dog, but our young mistress, and, strange to say, not as she usually appeared, but all blue, and her eyes glowing like red-hot coals. She seized the infant, and began to suck its blood. The Cheptchikha screamed out loudly, and rushed from the room to the loft, where the foolish woman, all trembling, hid herself. Our young mistress followed her, fastened upon, and began to bite her also. In the morning Cheptoun found his wife in the loft, bitten and bruised all over, and the next day she died. Only think what wonderful things happen sometimes! It matters very little whether one belongs to a great family or not—when one is a witch one is!"

Having related all this, Doroch sat down, quite satisfied with himself; and with his little finger began to clear out his pipe-bowl for a fresh supply. All then began to talk of the witch, and to relate anecdotes about her. To the house of one she had paid a visit in the form of a haystack, from a second had stolen his cap, from another his pipe; she had cut off the tresses of several girls in the village, and had quaffed buckets-full of blood from other of her father's peasants. At length the whole of the worthy company began to discover that they had gossiped long enough, and that it was already late in the night. They accordingly betook themselves to rest where they best could, some in the kitchen, some in the barns, and some in the courtyard.

"Come, Sir Thomas," said the old Cossack, addressing himself to the philosopher, "it is time for us to go to the dead body."

Accordingly, they all four—that is to say, he, the philosopher, Spirid, and Doroch—proceeded to the church, using their whips as they went along to keep off the numerous dogs that wandered about and endeavoured to bite them. Although the philosopher, before setting out, had not omitted to give a fillip to his courage through the medium of a good glass of brandy, he nevertheless felt a secret terror, which became stronger as they approached nearer to the church—the extraordinary stories he had that evening heard related having, not unnaturally, excited in a strong degree his imagination. They soon reached the church, the steps of which they all ascended; and after having seen the philosopher safely inside, the three Cossacks wished him good night, and, as they had been ordered, locked him in.

The philosopher remained alone—he yawned, stretched himself, and then began to survey the church. In the midst of it was the bier, covered with black; wax tapers with long wicks were burning before dusky images of saints, and threw a sombre light on some parts of the church, leaving however a great portion of it in total obscurity. The *iconostas*, or wooden division by which the nave was separated from the sanctuary, was lofty, and evidently of great age, as the carved work, which had once been gilt, was now bare in many places, the gilding having gradually fallen away. The faces of the saints had become quite black with age, and little more than the outline of the features could now be distinguished.

The philosopher looked carefully around him once more. "Well," he said to himself, "what is there to be afraid of?—no living being can enter here; and as for the dead and their ghosts, I know prayers enough to keep them off at arm's length. After all, it is nothing; so now for the prayers."

Approaching one of the choristers' stalls, he saw lying there a packet of wax tapers. "Come!" he thought, "at all events I can light up the old building, so that it shall be as bright inside as if it were midday. What a pity, though, that one can't smoke in a church!"

He then began to stick the tapers in all the cornices, on the balustrades, on the images—in short, wherever he could find a place for them—and the church was in a short time in a blaze of light, the upper part appearing by the contrast in still deeper gloom, and the blackened visages of the saints seeming to cast still more stern glances around them. He approached the bier—cast a terrified look upon the corpse—and closed his eyes with a shudder. What fearful, what dazzling beauty? He turned away his head, and sought to regain his place; but, from the strange curiosity which a man feels when under the impression of fear, he could not resist the impulse that induced him again to look, although agitated by the same convulsive shudder.

There was, in fact, something terrible in the proud and striking beauty of the corpse. It would not have caused him so much terror, probably, had the features been ugly; but nothing gloomy, nothing savouring of death, was to be seen in that face. It bore the stamp of life, and appeared to the philosopher to follow his movements even with closed eyes. He hastened to place himself in one of the stalls of the choir, opened his book, and to give himself courage, began to read in the loudest tones he could. His voice struck upon the old wooden walls of the church, so long abandoned to silence, without echo, without noise; his deep bass voice resounded amidst a deathly silence. He himself felt it to be strange and unnatural.

"What should I be afraid of!" he repeated to himself; "she cannot rise from her bier, for she will be too much afraid of the Holy Word—and what sort of a Cossack should I be to entertain fear! I have been drinking rather more than I ought, and that is the cause of my feeling afraid. Suppose I take a pinch of snuff—ah! excellent—what very good snuff!" Nevertheless, in turning over the leaves of the book, he could not help looking at the bier; and an internal voice seemed to whisper—"There she is! there!—see, she is getting up!—see, she lifts up her head!—look!"

The most profound silence, however, continued to prevail; the corpse remained immovable, the tapers threw out floods of light. The illuminated church, with the dead body in the middle, was in truth horrible to behold. Thomas began to chant, raising his voice in all its tones to drown the fear which, in spite of himself, he still felt, but continually turning his eyes towards the bier and involuntary asking himself this question—"Suppose she were to rise! suppose she were to rise!"

The corpse continued motionless; no sound was to be heard—not the least noise of living creature—not even a cricket; nothing but the occasional crackling of a taper, or the light dull sound of a drop of wax falling on the pavement.

"If she were to rise!"

She raised her head!

He looked on stupefied, and rubbed his eyes. "Can it be?—yes! She is no longer lying down; she is sitting on the bier!"

With a violent efforts he turned away his head, but in an instant after his eyes were again fixed on the corpse. She approached him slowly, with glazed eyes, but with extended arms, as if endeavouring to lay hold of some one. She came straight towards him. Confused, terrified, he yet hastened to trace with his finger a circle round the place where he stood, and began with violent effort to repeat the exorcisms which had been taught him by an old monk as safeguards against witches and evil spirits.

The corpse advanced to the verge of the circle, but evidently had not power to pass the invisible limit. She suddenly became blue and livid, like one who has been some days dead. Her features were hideous, her teeth chattered, and her glassy eyes were wide open; but she saw nothing. Trembling with rage, she moved round with extended arms, still seeking to lay hold of Thomas. At length she stopped, held up her finger in a menacing way, and then slowly drew back and again stretched herself upon the bier.

The philosopher remained aghast, unable to collect his senses, and casting looks of terror upon the long narrow coffin in which the corpse was now extended. Suddenly that coffin was lifted up, and, with a sharp shrill sound, rushed through the air, darting about all parts of the church, hovering over the very head of the poor philosopher, but unable to pass the circle traced around him. He repeated his exorcisms; the coffin precipitated itself with a loud sound into the middle of the church, and again became immovable. The corpse, now of a livid green, again rose up; but, as at this moment the crowing of a cock was heard in the distance, again replaced herself in the coffin, and all was still.

The philosopher felt his heart beat violently, large drops of perspiration hung upon his brow; but, reassured by the crowing of the cock, he resumed his task and courageously went on reading aloud. At daybreak a priest came to relieve him, attended by old Iavtoukh, who for the time filled the office of sexton.

For some time after his return to the house the philosopher was unable to sleep; at last, however, overcome by fatigue, he dropped off, and awoke only just in time for dinner. On opening his eyes, the adventure of the past night appeared to him only as a dream; and at dinner, after taking a glass of brandy to comfort him, he recovered his usual spirits, talking freely, and eating for his own share nearly the whole of a sucking-pig. Upon the subject of his visit to the church, however, he thought it better to say nothing; and to the numerous questions put by curious inquirers merely replied that "All sorts of things had taken place."

After dinner his usual good-humour was completely restored: he walked about the village, scraped acquaintance with all the inhabitants, and made himself so much at home as to be turned out of two houses where his attentions to the peasant girls were more free than polite. As evening approached, however, he became somewhat pensive. For some time before supper the young people of the house amused themselves by playing at *kragli*, a sort of game of skittles, in which, instead of balls, long sticks were used, and the winner had the privilege of riding on the back of the loser.

Near the threshold of the kitchen were collected the staid and elderly portion of the household, who, smoking their pipes, looked on gravely and remained unmoved when the younger ones were bursting their sides with laughter at some funny remark made by Spirid. In vain did our philosopher endeavour to take part in their games. One fixed and sombre idea had taken possession of his mind. He did all in his power to be merry during supper, but in proportion as the shades of night became deeper, so did terror steal over his soul.

"Come, sir," said the old Cossack, rising from table with Doroch; "come—it is time for us to proceed to business." They again conducted Thomas to the church as on the preceding evening, and again left him there alone, carefully locking the door after them. He again saw the dusky images of the saints, the old gilt mouldings, and the dark bier of the witch, immovable, silent, and menacing, in the middle of the church.

"Well," he murmured to himself, "I shall not feel surprised this time at all events; it's only the first time such a thing frightens me—yes, certainly the first time it is terrible, but after that it is not at all so—certainly, not at all." He hastened precipitately to his place, traced a circle with his finger around him, repeated some exorcisms, and then began to read in a loud voice, determined not to raise his eyes from the book, and not to pay attention to anything that passed.

An hour or more passed. Tired of his task he stopped, yawned, took out his snuff-box, but before taking a pinch from it, threw a timid glance at the bier. His very heart ceased to beat from sudden fright. Before him, close to him, at the very verge of the circle, was the horrible corpse, its dull glassy eyes fixed upon his. The poor student shuddered; an icy chill ran through his veins. Hastily casting down his eyes, he again began to recite prayers and exorcisms. He heard the corpse grinding its' teeth, he instinctively felt that its arms were stretched out to seize him; but on looking furtively around, he saw that it was not at the point immediately opposite to him, and that it appeared not to see him.

133

Suddenly it began to mutter in a low tone, and from its icy lips strange sounds came forth, the meaning of which he knew not, but felt they must be of fearful import. The thought crossed him that she was muttering incantations, and, in fact, a violent wind arose outside the church; a noise as of the rushing of a multitude of birds was heard, and it seemed to him that thousands of wings were beating against the glass, many claws clutching the window bars, and that a heavy mass was leaning against the door and making it groan upon its hinges. His heart beat violently, but he continued to recite his exorcisms, although with closed eyelids. A sharp cry was heard in the distance—it was cock-crow. The philosopher, worn out with emotion and fatigue, stopped, and drew a long breath.

Those who came to seek him in the morning found him half dead; leaning against a wall, he looked aghast with wide open eyes upon the Cossacks, who were at length obliged to carry him out of the church and to support him to the house. On his arrival there he shook himself, stared around, and called for a glass of brandy, which he swallowed at one gulp; then remarked, with a mysterious air, that "there was all sorts of wickedness in the world, and that sometimes the strangest things happened to one." Here he paused with a significant gesture, implying his determination to say nothing more, and, leaving his auditors in a state of gaping wonderment. Just at this moment a young kitchen-maid happened to pass by, a great *coquette* in her way, who addressed the philosopher with a smiling "good morning," and then, suddenly clasping her hands, exclaimed—"Gracious Heaven! what can have happened to you, sir?"

"Why, what is the matter, you silly girl?" he replied.

"What? why you have become quite grey!"

"Eh! eh! it is true," remarked Spirid; "your hair is as grey as old Iavtoukh's!"

At these words the philosopher rushed into the kitchen, where he had seen a little triangular piece of looking-glass with sundry flowers around it, the property of the *coquettish* kitchen nymph; and true enough, on looking in it, he saw with horror that his hair had indeed turned grey! He hung down his head, reflected deeply, and then said, "I will go at once to the *centenier*, tell him all, and state that I positively will not read any more prayers, let him send me to Kiew if he likes." He then went straight to the house. The *centenier* was sitting in his room, in the same place and in the same state of deep and painful reflection. His face bore the same expression of hopeless grief, and his pale and sunken cheek showed that he had taken little or no nourishment; he might, indeed, have been taken for a marble statue.

"Good morning," he said, on seeing Thomas, who had remained at the door cap in hand; "well, how do you get on; everything is in order, I believe?"

"Oh yes, sir, in order indeed—there are such goings on there, that the only thing one can do is to take up one's hat and run off as quickly as possible."

"How is that—what do you mean?"

"Why, your daughter, sir—certainly she was a lady of noble extraction, and no one can say anything against her—but I hope you will not be angry. Heaven rest her soul?"

"Well, what about my daughter?"

"Why, she must have made a bargain with the devil; she frightens people so, that prayers are of no use whatever."

"Read them—read them nevertheless—there must have been some good reason for her wishing you to come! She was careful of her soul, was my poor little one, and no doubt was anxious for prayers to keep away all unholy influences."

" Sir, I swear to you that it is beyond my strength."

"Read, read, my dear fellow," continued the *centenier*, in a persuasive tone; "you have only one night more to pass there; you will perform a pious deed, and shall be well recompensed."

"It is useless, sir; whatever recompense you may propose, I cannot and will not recite any more prayers."

"Listen, mister philosopher," said the *centenier*, whose voice now became loud and stem. "I am not fond of these nonsensical tales; you may do as you please at home at your college, but not here. If I have you flogged, it will not be after the same fashion

135

as your rector. Do you know what *kantchouks,* (small leather whips), are?"

"I should think so," replied the philosopher, casting down his eyes; "everybody knows what they are—when there are many of them they are intolerable."

"Yes, but you don't know how my people use them on another's back," said the *centenier,* rising abruptly, his face assuming a fierce and haughty expression indicative of his character when not overcome by grief; "my people begin by giving a good warming, then throw a little brandy on to cool, and then begin warming again. Come, come, sir, do your duty, or you will repent it! Do it well, and you shall have a thousand *ducats.*"

The philosopher retired, murmuring to himself, "There is no joking with this fellow; but he is mistaken if he thinks I am going to stay. I'll give him the slip in such a manner that not even his dogs shall be able to find scent of me." He now determined to take to flight, awaiting for this purpose the dinner hour, immediately after which all the household were in the habit of betaking themselves to the haylofts, there to sleep with open mouths, and to snore and snort with a degree of vigour that might have induced people to think the place a nursery for young steam engines.

The hour at last came, and even Iavtoukh stretched himself at full length in the sun and closed his eyes. Treading softly as a cat, our philosopher stole out into the garden, whence he thought he might more readily make his way into the fields. This garden was as usual neglected and overrun with weeds, and consequently better suited to his secret enterprise; with the exception of one narrow beaten path from the house, the ground was covered with cherry trees which were growing quite wild, with elder trees, and thistles that raised their downy heads above the other weeds, the whole interwoven with a network of ivy.

Beyond the hedge by which the garden was encircled, was a complete forest of heaths, into which probably no one had ever penetrated, and which would have laughed to scorn the attempts of any scythe. When about to leap over the hedge his teeth chattered and his heart beat so violently, that he himself was alarmed at the emotion; the skirts of his long gown appeared to have become fastened to the ground, as if they had been pinned down, and he fancied he heard a shrill voice at his ear crying out, "Where are you going?"

He plunged into the wilderness of heaths, and began running as fast as he could, stumbling however every minute over old stumps of trees and molehills. He now saw that once out of the heaths he would only have pass over a field, beyond which was an expanse covered with thick brambles in which he might hide with safety, and which, as he conjectured, would lead him dose to the road to Kiew. He cleared the field rapidly, and soon reached the brambles, through which he made his way with much difficulty, leaving upon each bush a portion of his caftan. All at once he came upon a dear open space, through which ran a streamlet pure and fresh; and throwing himself down he drank long and hearty draughts, to extinguish the intolerable thirst he felt.

"What delicious water," he exclaimed, wiping his lips; "it might be as well to stay here; but no, I had better run on, perhaps I am already pursued." These words were repeated, as if by some one standing over him; and raising his head abruptly, there sure enough was Iavtoukh.

"Cursed Iavtoukh!" he muttered to himself; "how I should like to take you by the heels and dash your ugly head against the trees."

"You might have spared yourself such a long round," said the Cossack, very quietly; "you had better have come by the direct path from the stables, as I did, and see—what a pity! you have torn your *caftan*; it's not bad stuff—how much did it cost the *archine?* But come, we have had walking enough; let us return to the house."

The philosopher with a very sheepish look, turned back. "It is of no use," he thought, "that confounded witch is determined to have me! But after all what have I to fear—am I not a Cossack? I have got through two nights, and Heaven will help me to get over the third. That cursed witch certainly must have committed a great many crimes, or the Evil One would never protect her so."

His mind occupied with similar reflections, he returned to the house, and begged Doroch, who, thanks to the butler's influence, had sometimes access to the cellars, to bring him a bottle of brandy; to this they both sat down, and soon swallowed so large a portion that the philosopher at last started suddenly to his feet, calling out, "Music!—I want music—bring me some music!" and without waiting for it he at once, in the middle of the courtyard, began to dance the *tropak,* and continued to do so for so long a time, that the people of the household, who had formed a circle round him as customary, at last became tired of the performance and went away in disgust. He at length gave over, and fell asleep in the same place so soundly that they were obliged to throw a bucket of water over him, to rouse him up for supper. During that meal he did nothing but boast of what Cossacks were, and to assert that he feared nothing in the world.

"Come," said Iavtoukh, "it is time; let us go,"

"A lighted match to your tongue, (common Southern Russian expression), old boor," thought the philosopher, who however arose, saying, "Let us go."

On their way to the church he kept repeatedly looking from one side to the other, and endeavouring to enter into conversation with ,his conductors. Iavtoukh, however, remained silent, and even Doroch appeared little inclined to talk. The night was dark and dismal, the howling of the wolves was heard in the distance, and even the barking of the dogs seemed to have something lugubrious in its sound.

"One might fancy," at length exclaimed Doroch, "that those are not wolves that are howling, but howlers of a different description."

Iavtoukh kept silent, and the philosopher made no reply. They at last reached the church, and passed under the old wooden arches, whose decay bore proof of the little care the *centenier* took of his own soul. Iavtoukh and Doroch went their way as usual, and the philosopher remained alone. All around him was precisely in the same state as on the previous day; he paused for a moment; the bier was still immovable in the midst of the church. "I shall not be afraid—I shall not be afraid!" he repeated to himself; and, having drawn around him the protecting circle, he began hastily to recite exorcisms.

A horrible silence prevailed; the tapers burnt with a dull, yellow, flickering light that but partially illumined the church. The philosopher turned first one page, then another; then discovered that he was reading anything but what was in the book before him. He crossed himself and began to chant some prayers; this reassured him a little. He again began to read with rapidity, and page after page followed in quick succession; when suddenly, in the midst of the appalling silence, the iron bands of the coffin burst asunder with a loud report, and the corpse arose, still more frightful than on the previous occasion; its teeth chattered loudly, convulsive twitchings agitated its lips, and the conjurations to which it gave utterance were broken by sharp, harsh cries.

A whirlwind arose in the church; the holy images, the broken windows, were dashed violently to the ground; the door was torn from its hinges, and an innumerable multitude of monsters rushed into the holy precincts. A confused noise of wings flapping, and of bodies clashing against each other, filled the church; and this crowd ran, clambered, flew around it, in search of the philosopher.

The last fumes of drunkenness had now evaporated from his brain; he made repeated signs of the cross, he stammered forth prayers; but, while so doing, still heard the crowd of monsters seeking him, brushing him with the tips of their wings, with the ends of their claws and of their horrible tails. He had not courage to look at them attentively; he saw but one enormous monster that filled nearly the whole of the side of the church opposite to him. It was covered with long dishevelled hair, through which two large eyes with lids slightly raised stared with a fixed and strong stare. Above him, hovering in the air, appeared something like an enormous bladder furnished with innumerable lobster claws and scorpion tails, to which fragments of black earth were hanging. All looked for the philosopher, all sought for him; but could neither see nor touch him while within the magic circle,

"Let the King of the Gnomes be brought here," exclaimed the corpse; "let him come here."

At these words all became hushed, and profound silence now reigned within the church. Suddenly a wild howling was heard from afar, then heavy steps were heard near the church. Throwing a glance around, the philosopher saw that they were bringing in a kind of man of short stature, broad and clumsy in form, and with crooked legs. He was covered with, and soiled by, earth; his feet and hands resembled knotty roots; he walked with difficulty, and stumbled at every step; the long lashes of his closed eyelids fell to the ground, and Thomas saw with terror that his face was of iron. He was led, supported under each arm, exactly opposite the spot where the philosopher stood.

"Lift up my eyelids—I see not," said the King of the Gnomes, in a deep, subterraneous tone. And the crowd pressed around to lift them up.

"Look not," said an internal voice to the philosopher; but he had not strength to resist, and looked.

"There he is!" cried out the King of the Gnomes, pointing with his finger.

The obscene crowd threw themselves upon the unfortunate philosopher; bewildered, terrified, he fell and died on the instant. At this moment the shrill crow of the cock was heard—it was the second, the gnomes had not paid attention to the first. In their haste and terror they threw themselves precipitately and in confusion against the doors and windows, in order to depart; but it was no longer time, and they remained fixed to the places through which they had endeavoured to escape.

The priest, who came in the morning to read the prayers for the dead, durst not pass the threshold of the church, which remained thus forever.

A Twopenny Ghost Story
For Certain Little Boys

It was not a very long time ago that a little boy was passing along a certain street in London, which leads down to a great hospital, where other little boys live, who have no fathers, and whose mothers seldom come to see them. The name of the street is Lamb's Conduit-street, and the name of the little boy was Harry Summers.

Of course it was very natural for little Harry to look into the shop windows, where books with pretty pictures, or grand pictures, or touching pictures, stood; and of course, also, it was natural in him to wait and wonder at the toy-shops, wherein King Nutcracker, with such very great jaws and great staring eyes, stood, and where certain balloons, and bats, and balls, and cricket-stumps, and ninepins were all ranged; not to mention, also, the little fleecy dogs, with bright red cloth tongues, bead eyes, and a bark as much like a feeble puff through a penny trumpet as anything could be.

But what struck Harry the most was a long box, like a domino-box, in which there lay two very pretty painted fish, which had apparently not long been caught, for they had pieces of hooks, or of iron pins, sticking out of their mouths, and of these Harry knew the use; for these fish would swim in a basin of water, and when a little boy or girl dropped down the clumsy hook into the water, the fish were, somehow or other, drawn to it, and they swam towards it, and touched it with their bits of iron, and so were drawn up and caught.

Well, Harry went on, wondering, and longing to have some of these, but not envying those who had them, being a good boy, and easily contented with his trap, bat, and ball, and his fine kite at home. So he left that wonderful toy-shop, and went on.

He had not gone very far, and had not done laughing at the cowardice of a great rough curly dog, which ran away from a very fierce little terrier, when he came to a shop which was almost as wonderful as the toy-shop. It was that of a tea-dealer and grocer, and in the window all sorts of pleasant things were to be seen.

There were rich pots of marmalade and jams, piled upon one another in such a quantity, that Harry thought that all the boys of his school, if they were to carry one each away, would not be able to exhaust the shop. Then, in another place were brown Normandy pippins, with their rough coats and their flat tops, looking very nice and homely. Then raisins and almonds, such boxes of the one and such quantities of this other, that Harry felt that even he would have been a very long time in finishing them; and then, besides all these, as if these were not enough for a moderate grocer, there was a perfect horn of plenty of sugar-candy, and a profusion of boxes of French plums, cases of tea, tilted on one side, as if they had been just overturned, while from their mouths the fragrant, curly, green or black leaf poured out.

The grocer was, and must have been, a very rich man—so Harry thought—for besides all these treasures, and besides, also, all the ripe Portugal grapes, red and white, and the boxes of figs which were, beside them, in the middle of the window was a bowl of bright penny-pieces, which twinkled in the sun, and looked as if they were gold. Little Harry never saw such new pennies before, and was quite astonished at the grocer for keeping them there; yet there they were; and the man was not content in piling the bowl up in a pyramid-like form, but several had dropped over; as if this rich grocer did not care for penny-pieces, but could afford to let them lie in his window in that manner.

Now the more Harry looked at these penny-pieces, the more he wanted them: that is, not all of them, but one of them; and he declared to himself that he should only like to take one home to show his sister. So he looked and looked, and thought, and put his hand in his pocket, and felt sixpence there, which his mother had given him the day before. He had serious thoughts of going in, and asking the grocer if he would give him a penny-piece for the sixpence; but as a spruce young mechanic looks better than an old and worn-out nobleman, so the sixpence looked so thin and worn, and old and poor, that little Harry was absolutely ashamed to go and ask such a favour.

Now it happened that the grocer had a very smart young fellow, a shopman, who used sometimes to walk to the door and ask the customers to walk in and purchase. He had a great deal to say, and he said it; and he was quite a favourite with his master on account of the number of customers which he coaxed into his shop. He came out directly he saw Harry, and spoke to him confidently, saying—

"Now, my little man, what would you like? Those are very nice figs;" and, as he said this, he looked—the sly fellow—at the sixpence in little Harry's hand, and said, "And I'll tell you what we'll do,"—he said "*we*," because he meant himself, and the master, and the shop, and all in fact, he was such a great fellow,—"and I'll tell you what we'll do. We'll give you half a pound of those nice figs to take home to your mamma, and a bright new penny-piece into the bargain, for that sixpence."

Harry jumped at the very idea, and thought what a lucky young fellow he was, and went inside at once, and was all of a tremble till he had the packet of figs tied up in a neat parcel by the generous young shopman, in one hand, and the new penny-piece, put into a little envelope with the grocer's name upon it. Just as if it had been made on purpose, in his pocket. He could not eat the figs for thinking of his penny-piece, and quite surprised his mother by his generosity. Indeed, that kind lady was so touched by her son's kindness, that she immediately gave him another sixpence, and—a great part of the figs—just enough for him to eat without making him ill—as a reward. And further, she told his father and his brothers and sister what a good boy he was.

Now Harry *was* a good boy, and did not like to be praised for that which he did not quite deserve; and when his mother said, "And to think that he did not eat one of the figs!" little Harry told her how the shopman proposed it, and how he had got the bright penny-piece, and he showed the little envelope with the grocer's name on it, where the bright penny lay quite comfortably. It was his father's turn to laugh now, and he laughed out with a great loud laugh, and called Harry to him, and gave him a kiss on his forehead, for he was more fond of kissing Harry's little sister than he was Harry, and told him that he was indeed a good boy for speaking the truth; and looked at his penny, and offered him sixpence for it; and when Harry would not take it, he called him a block- head, and gave him the sixpence.

But all this time Harry's mother looked rather disappointed, and he, who was now rich and could afford it,, therefore, walked up to her and offered her the penny-piece and the sixpence, to make her smile. So she smiled, and told him to take them away, and put them in his money-box. Little Harry at once did this, and unlocked the box and put the two sixpences together, and the bright penny-piece in another partition, with an old, smooth, dark penny, nearly black, and very ugly, which Harry had had for ever so long a time. When he saw the two pennies together, Harry despised the old one, and took the bright penny out, and put it with the sixpences; and he was not even satisfied then, for he took it out again to look at.

It was such a fine thing, so thick, so heavy, so bright, so sharp in its stamp. It had letters all round it, and on one side there was the head of a very good and handsome lady, who is our queen, with a quantity of words in Latin,, which Harry could not make out. And on the other side there was Britannia with her shield and trident, looking very firm, and with her shield leaning against the rock upon which she sat, and upon it were the crosses of St. Andrew and St. George. Underneath this grand lady's feet were three flowers, the rose, the shamrock, and the thistle, which, as Harry had heard tell, were symbols of England, Ireland, and Scotland; and in her hand was a trident, which showed, said the people, that she ruled the sea; but the reason of her bearing the trident, the sceptre of the ancient god of the sea, was at the time not very plain to Harry.

The old smooth penny-piece had a face upon it too, but it was not so very pretty as the face of the queen; and as for the. Britannia on the other side, it was an old worn-out figure, with no helmet or armour on her breast, and looking like a very poor thing, in comparison with the other. So Harry kept looking at his bright penny-piece till it was time to go to bed, and when it was so, he put away his bright penny-piece with the sixpences, and leaving the old one quite solitary by itself, little Harry went to bed, and kept on thinking of his fine new penny till he went to sleep.

He had not been long asleep when he had a dream. Somehow or other—for he did not know how—the bright penny-piece came out of his box and stood by his bed. Although he knew it was the penny, yet it was only the beautiful lady Britannia who stood near him, her bright helmet shining, her armour twinkling, and her scarlet robe rustling as it fell over her shoulder like the robe of a queen. She held her shield, also of bright steel, but painted beautifully in the centre, on her hand, and her arms were bare and beautifully white and round, and looked like those of a marble goddess. Little Harry was quite charmed with her, and at the same time quite alarmed.

Presently he heard the lid of the little money-box lift up and shut down again, and then the little old lady from the other penny-piece, came also, and stood by him. There never was such a contrast as between these two ladies. The one was old, worn, and infirm, and looked more like a shadow than anything else; the other stood upright and firm, and looked like a queen. The shield of the eldest was rusty, and it had nothing on it; her trident also had lost its head, and looked more like an old stick; that of the youngest was sharp and dreadful to look at, being so glittering and pointed, and her shield was painted and ornamented, and its bright edge glittered like a looking- glass. Her robes also were beautiful and cleanly, and hung with ample and majestic folds; but those of the eldest clung round her worn body, and looked almost as shadowy as herself.

Harry had not done wondering when they both looked at him, and spoke.

"I," said the first—the bright, glittering, beautiful lady, who looked so much like Britannia on a Christmas transparency,—"I am the genius of the new penny-piece; I am untouched, unsullied, pure. No dirty hands have handled me. I am fit to be placed in the cabinet of a *savant*—to be examined by the glass of a numismatist."

Little Harry rather opened his eyes at the very big words which the little spirit spoke; but he thought, and perhaps rightly, that fine words and fine clothes should go together, so he said nothing. The fine lady continued, with a pretty curl of disdain upon her beautifully cut lips, sweeping away, with a fine free dash, her crimson robe, which fell heavily, it may be, for it was rich and new, a *leetle*—just a little—too near the worn old figure by her side.

"I have said that I am unsullied. I am pure, I am absolutely unused to the world's ways; but I know my own value."

"Certainly," thought Harry, "and it may be," says the reader, "a little above it;" but then grand people, just fresh from the mint, frequently mistake a little in that way."

"I have never," she said, "been given away for water-cresses, nor for penny loaves, nor for hearthstone, nor Lucifer-matches; no, nor for cat's meat.'"

The withering way in which she said the last word was a wonder to hear. The word took effect like a chain shot; the poor ragged, withered figure seemed to quiver, to shrink, to bend under it, and shook and trembled so much that little Harry mixed up some pity with the great deal of contempt which he felt for her; and very properly so too, for little boys like Harry are not bound, no, nor sometimes taught nowadays, to feel any reverence for poverty and age, especially when accompanied by so foolish a thing as lowliness or meekness—though, to be sure, the author of this foolish (but true) story has met with an obscure book which speaks of poverty as a blessing, and of age as an honour.

"I have never," continued the imperial little puppet, "been tossed by the boys; never been dropped into beggars' hats, nor thrown to serenaders, nor to tumbling clowns; no, nor paid away for lollipops, sugar-sticks, withered apples, and Boneypart's ribs; and therefore," she continued, with much dignity, tucking her pretty little waxen arms *akimbo*, and making a low curtsy to Harry,—"and therefore, I will thank you, sir, not to confine me in the same apartment with such a—a person (how cuttingly she said the word!) as the present."

Harry thought that the word "apartment" was rather a grand term for his money-box; but the word was so suited to the speaker's lips, that he could not feel annoyed with it; and, to be sure, the lady was so fresh and *riante* that she might well have claimed the precedence she did, and by a brevet rank have been placed with the new shillings and sixpences, and have had a quantity of bright threepenny-pieces to reign over as her subjects (sometimes, you know, a good subject is worth three times as much as a monarch, for which fact we refer to the present Spanish currency), or have been moved up higher and have consorted with the sovereigns and half-sovereigns, had Harry's money-box contained any.

The little withered woman now thought it was her turn to speak. Twice she tried, and twice "*tears, intermixed with sighs, found out their way.*" Hallo! I fancy I have met that combination of sounds before. Oh! Mr. Milton, is it? I thank you. You are surprised at being quoted in a spirit-story. Well, so am I.

At length a little squeaky voice, but very, very sad—squeaky, I said; for poverty does not always (and age very seldom) speak in grand solemn tones. At length this voice began, and somewhat, to Harry's ears, in this way:—"I am old—very old, and very weak and poor; I am very nearly worn out."

"They always begin in this way," cried the imperial figure; "as if we cared for their catalogue of sorrows—not a bit."

"It is quite true what her majesty hath said. I have been in very sorry company," said the figure; "but I suppose it was my fate. I was born a very great while ago; I have seen a great deal of life; I am very tired of it, and am nearly worn out."

"And a good job too, I should think, when you are quite so," said the other lady, very proudly; "we have really, nowadays, a great deal too many poor people about. What they mean by it I do not know. They pester us in the streets; they look at us in a hungry way when we go near any bakers' shops, or if we happen to step into the confectioner's to take an ice; they bother us with violets in the early spring and winter, as if we cared for violets—a camellia only suits *my* hair. They trouble us in many, many ways.

"On opera nights the real poor run along by the side of our carriages, pushing at the glass windows as if they would break them, with programmes and words of the opera; as if we cared for the words of an opera. We only go to hear the music, you know. As for the streets, I am sure it is quite dreadful; because you really now cannot step from your jeweller's into your brougham but what a pale face haunts you with an impudent look, as much as to say, 'What business have you to buy that trinket whilst *I* starve?' A pretty pass it has come to, forsooth."

Here the figure tossed her robe again, and swept away farther from the other, in great disdain. It is to be observed that she talked very highly for only a penny-piece; but a great many more people in this funny world talk of broughams than ride in them; and the writer has noted, that many a penny-piece lady in society talks quite as loudly as if she were a half-crown or five shillings at least.

"I was born as well as that lady," continued the worn figure. "A duchess was my great-grandmother. Frances Stewart, her Grace of Richmond—a great lady in the time of Charles the Second[4]—I claim as my progenitrix."

---

4. The spirit, perhaps, alludes to the fact of the figure of Britannia on our copper coinage being originally modelled from the august lady mentioned.

The figure looked more proudly as she said this, and the other lady opened her eyes a little.

"I was born in the Mint, and was as bright and as beautiful as the lady here when I first saw the world—perhaps more so. I was more like my great-grandmother, I am sure. My trident was unbroken, my shield fresh and new, my robe unworn. You see how ragged it is now.

"The first few years of my life were perhaps the saddest. I saw the light when old King George the Third was a young man. We call him old now; it is hard to think that he was once young. I bear his head upon me as a mark that I was his liege slave.

"A good citizen of London, going to change a note, brought me from the bank; and, with a new sixpence and a threepenny-piece, I was given in a little yellow canvas bag to his son. The little boy was never tired at looking at me. Master Harry; for I was bright then, and beautiful, and shone like gold, or like my sister there. The little boy would take me out with him; and one day, I and my companions in the yellow bag were snatched from his hand.

"There was an immense hue and cry, a 'Halloa! stop thief!' a scuffle, a hurry, and a great deal of running; and presently two stout fellows, in flannel coats and with great flopped hats, and with stockings rolled up above the knees of their breeches ("What a word, to be sure!" cried the pretty lady, hiding her face with her shield) came up, holding a pale young fellow, thin, gaunt, and ragged, by both his arms. They brought back the purse; and presently a tipstaff came and took the young thief, who was only twenty years of age, the nurse-maid, and my young master to the magistrate.

"The thief was at his penitentials at once, and cried, and talked about a starving wife and child; but they committed him, and hauled him to prison at once. There had been a great stir made about robberies, and the clumsiness of the watch; and they were determined to make an example. My young master cried very much for his purse and penny-piece; but they kept that as proof; for I was the only piece the nurse could swear to.

"Poor fellow! what he said was true. His wife and child were starving; but they did not think that any excuse; and one morning the young fellow was brought out, with four others—one highwayman, one forger, a burglar, and a woman who had stolen a piece of meat—and was with them hanged till he was dead!"

"What, for stealing ten pence!" cried Harry, indignantly.

"Ah, poor fellow! Yes—they did so in those days. Poor man!"

"What, pity a thief?" cried the duchess-like lady; "Oh my!"

"I am not the only one who has taken pity on a thief," returned the other calmly.

"I was next changed away (for I did *not* return to young master) for some strong waters, by one of the watchmen; and I fell into the hands of a dashing young publican, at whose house some of the gentlemen of the road used to call. The highwayman robbed a stage-coach, took all the money from a Quaker; and, out of a careless good nature, gave me, with a handful of others, into the outstretched hands of a poor usher, who had ridden up to London in search of employment, in the basket of the coach.

"Just like those wicked wretches. They take sovereigns, and notes, and gold watches, and what not, and then give away penny-pieces in charity!"

"Like other people, too," returned the ragged figure. "I was given up by the usher, in charge to a man who kept a cellar in Monmouth-street, near Seven-dials, wherein he sold boiled beef, and gave as large a dinner, as his customers could eat, for sixpence. I was not long in his possession; nor need I have been, for the greasy hands of the Irish waitress took away all my brightness, and I had already been knocked about a good deal."

"I dare say," said her companion, in high disdain; "then you should take care what company you keep."

"Wait," said the other,—" wait till you get out into the world. You will be rubbed against strange companions. You will not always be able to keep your freshness and your polish; you will have to mourn over a change day by day, over loss of high looks, high thoughts, and a brave, fresh mind, which once thought it could conquer everything. You do not know what a little rubbing with the world does for the like of us."

"Nor do I want, madam!"

"Perhaps not," said the other sadly; "but want it or not. Time brings it to all of us, soon enough. Heaven knows.

"I was next given by the Irish maid to a very thin poor gentleman, who wore a silver-hilted sword, tin shoe-buckles, a brown wig, and a hat with some copper lace on it. By an agreement, he limited his supply of meat each day to threepence, and I noticed that when I fell into his pocket, that I had only two other pennies, a penknife, and a tobacco-box to rattle against. He was a poet, and wrote for the magazines of the period; and filled the pocket-books, published then, with those beautiful verses and charades which were all at the end. He made a very poor living at it, though, and often slept on the bulks at Covent-garden, with one or two other gentlemen of his craft, who would laugh and talk with each other very bravely and beautifully; never railing against Fortune, except to call her a jade, and to quote poetry against her. When imprisoned in his pocket, I used to think him mad.

"He kept me a long time, though; for taking me out by the moonlight to pay for some tobacco, I looked so new that he rubbed me on his coat-sleeve, and said he would keep me as a pocket-piece for good luck, so that he might always have a coin about him. He did so for a long time; but being at last lodged with the poor debtors in the Fleet Prison, he tossed me away, a halfpenny at a venture, with a Fleet parson, just to kill time.

"The parson, who was not then much plagued with marriages, the fees of which alone paid him, gave me away to a turnkey for a tin of beer, and the turnkey gave me to a poor prisoner who was starving there, to buy a penny loaf. I do not know whether the man was too weak to live or whether the bread choked him. Certainly he died with a part of it in his mouth. I went away to a baker's boy, who, having been given a money-box, had commenced saving. He kept me prisoner many years, till he came to man's estate, and then I was changed into other moneys; but I was black, battered, and bruised by constant shaking and moving in that little miser's box."

"Oh! what a vulgar story yours is," cried the lady, yawning.

"I will not trouble you long," said the other. "I have been the first penny which commenced the fortune of a *millionaire*. I have been the last which a spendthrift, who has run through an ancient estate, and has brought an honourable house to nothings has spent. I have been good, and been the means of good; I have dropped from the hands of sainted charity into a beggar's hat. I have been part of the sum which bought a human soul; I have bribed innocence, and corrupted virtue."

"Here's a pretty confession to make, quotha!"

"True it is so," said the old woman; "but, nevertheless, I have LIVED!"

As she spoke the magical word, she seemed to grow a finer, stronger woman. True, her face was worn, and her helmet and shield bent; but her form seemed stranger and more shapely, whilst the brightness of the other grew more like tinsel glitter. The old figure did indeed remind Harry of a picture of a duchess, and he did not doubt the old lady's assertion about her maternal great-grandmother.

"I have lived!" cried the old Britannia. "I have seen life, its joys and sorrows. I have been the happy coin given by a hardworking mechanic to his child as a Christmas-box. I have been the treasured penny spent at last to buy an orange to moisten a mother's dying lips. I have been portion of the washed coin brought by obsequious waiters at a white-bait dinner, for young gentlemen to throw to the little wretches who dive for coppers in the black mud of the Thames. I have travelled from London to the country. I have been in the pocket of a plough-boy bard, and have been spent at fairing times and market days as a penny should be.

"'*Spend and be spent*,' that is the rule of life; what else do we live for? Better rub than rust, a great deal; better be worn away than be eaten by *verdigris* and poisoned copperas, and such rust as too much rest *must* bring to all."

It was perfectly amazing to see what a change came over little Harry's vision. Here was the bright penny-piece, absolutely looking ashamed before the old worn one, and the latter holding herself upright like a queen.

"Let us live; let us rub and get shabby, if you will," she continued, "rather than do nothing. I declare I would not be a lazy drone for half the world. Fine clothes, i' faith; we all wear the same clothes when we come out of the mint, the workers and the wearers; and for myself, I would rather rub and rub, and wear and wear, month by month and day by day, assisting Jack, offending Tom, living by Harry, and keeping Ned; '*live and let live*,' you know, young woman."

Prodigious! she absolutely dared to poke the finely-dressed creature with her old worn trident; whereat the other shrunk away, I promise you.

"Than do nothing all my days but be looked at, be worth nothing but to wear fine clothes; make nothing but work for others; and say nothing but talk about weariness and *ennui*,—that's not the life for me, not if I were to be shut up in the velvet-lined mahogany cabinet of a connoisseur, with a parlour to myself; nay, nor even if, like a holy recluse, I were to be closed in the foundation of a church, harmless, quiet, and apart from all.

"I am for a life of activity," she said, with a smile; "for I am a circulating Medium, I am; and so, goodbye."

Tingle, tingle, clatter and roll. Then a little jump and a slam, and the two penny spirits are shut in the money-box.

Harry opened his eyes—it was dark. He shut them for a time, opened them again—it was light and morning.

He did not caress his fine penny so much as before; and whether or no he absolutely saw what I tell you he did, and heard all I have related, I do not know; but I know this, he was ever after more lenient to worn faces and old clothes, and did not think much of a brand new penny-piece, knowing that in the eyes of the wise, and of the Great Master of the Mint, it is of just the same value as, and of no more than, the shabbiest old penny in the kingdom, provided *always* that the metal of the latter be good.

Snap-Dragon

Mr. Snatchit—the Public!

Excellent Public—Mr. Snatchit!

The introduction being thus, and the introducer beings on the authority of his cheque-book, correct, the first thing Mr. Septimus Snatchit would have done would have been to ask whether he could do anything for the public; for, presuming a little employment—bringing in say only fifteen *per cent.*—*could* be got out of the public, Snatchit was the man.

Snatchit was the man, sir. Totally unaided industry, sir—unwearied exertion, sir—undoubted integrity, sir—immense talents, sir—ending in unexampled prosperity, sir! Do you want any more of that sort of writing, Mr. Public? because, if you do, read the next account, or the last account, of the next, or last, testimonial to be given, or given, to the next, or last, successful man. You will hear it all over again. Snatchit had heard it a dozen times, and said, "He didn't want to hear no more on't, dash 'em."

He was the seventh son of the Rev. —— Snatchit, who had in due course been snatched away. As the family were good, the reverend gentleman had provided for them according to his means, which became each day small by degrees and beautifully less. Therefore, whilst Snatchit Primus and Secundus came in for pretty good things, little Septimus inherited the usually light heart and thin inexpressibles which accompany poverty.

Mr. Sep's earliest ideas were bent upon making the latter very much thicker; and in the course of a long life he never neglected his own interest, nor did an action which did not bring him either an ultimate or a proximate advantage. That was all his art. That rule was alone his magic staff—his divining-rod, by adhering to which, the said garments grew thicker and better, and the heart grew heavier every day. Septimus was now the richest of the brothers, and he felt his heavy heart give a feeble leap of triumphant pleasure every time he thought on't.

The Rev. Snatchit, *père*, had been long ago dead; so the brothers stood thus:—Primus in the church, the successor of his father; Secundus was in the law; Tertius in the army, crotchety but generous, and on half-pay by this time; Quartus was a physician, not very clever, nor with a very first-rate practice; poor little Quintus, the pet of the brothers, had died out in India; Sextus was a merchant, who had unfortunately just failed, but was now going on again; and Septimus we have introduced to the public.

So they all agreed, these brothers, between them, to spend Christmas together at the old parsonage-house at Much-Harold, Bucks, which was not a mile away from Sep's bank in the town. For Sep had opened a bank, and used to discount the farmers' bills, and lend money, and advance Jones's savings to Brown's necessities, and to make money out of both. That was unwearied industry and undoubted integrity combined, you know.

When I say " all agreed," Sep did not agree. He did not agree, although the bland Primus, in a white neck-cloth, and the fierce Tertius, in military undress, both begged him to come.

"It was the last time they might meet on earth," said Primus.

"And theme is a question about us all meeting in Heaven," cried the brusque Tertius.

"Hush!" said the clergyman; "you will offend our brother."

"Oh! I meant myself, upon my shoe-sole I did," said ingenuous Miles.

"It is of no use, brothers. You may all go home. I will not come. I am busy."

"But on Christmas Day?"

"Well, that aren't Sunday, is it?" snarled Septimus to Primus.

"Come along, captain," said the clergyman, hopelessly; "it is of no use."

"Yes, and a nice lot we are," said the soldier, when in the street. "You make your little catechists say hymns, '*birds in their little nests agree,*' &c. &c., and here's an example of brotherly love we set 'em."

"Try him again then," retorted the parson, "with the youngsters; and now come and see the new screen in the church, and look at the way in which we are decorating it."

So in ten minutes' time Septimus was forgotten, and the clergyman and the soldier were standing, like green men of the woods, up to their knees in bunches of ivy and holly, giving directions, and aiding the decorators of the Christmas church. The captain had his huge campaigning knife in his hand, and was cutting and snipping away, and picking out the fairest branches and the reddest bunches of berries to stand foremost.

Septimus was tried again. His nephews tried him; but they so offended him that he revoked his intention of giving them a bright half-crown each, and put the money back into the bank. His nieces tried him, and were thoroughly put to the blush by being asked whether their fine ribbons were paid for; and last of all the babies tried him, with one little lisping thing for a spokeswoman.

"Come, Uncle Sep," she cried; "do come and play at snapdragons."

"Take her away, woman," he cried to the nurse. "I do believe that my relations want to insult me. Snap-dragons, indeed! Snap-dragons!"

So on Christmas Day it happened that the family was divided, after all, and that the larger part dined at the Parsonage, and the smaller—Mr. Septimus himself—at his own little house, in his strong room at the back of the bank.

You may make a very pleasant family party when there are plenty of young cousins. There will be flirting, laughing and talking, and mistletoe in abundance. The best mistletoe in the world is the family mistletoe. So the families of Primus, Secundus, &c. &c., thought, and plenty of fun they had, and after that, snap-dragon.

It so happened that at the very time at which the snap-dragon began at the Parsonage, Mr. Septimus crawled, very cold and miserable indeed, to his bed. He had been thinking all day of his relations, and was much more sorry than he dared to own to himself, because he had refused them. He had even opened a bottle of brandy, which some one of his brothers had sent him, and had mixed himself some spirit and water. He had drunk this, and then, as we say, crawled to bed. He then, having a little table near his side, reached his hand for the candle, and with a feeble puff blew it out.

No such thing! He blew the whole room into an illumination. He blew a party into the room. He blew a feast on the table—such a feast! He blew wine into the decanters; punch into an old china bowl; blancmange into some plates. That puff of old Septimus Snatchit's was more efficacious than the most elaborated puff ever blown by the most successful of modern tradesmen. He not only blew a variety of good things everywhere and all over the place, but he blew things into the room which never were there before.

For instance, he blew over the mantel-shelf a splendid picture—a copy, no doubt, as it was quite modern—of "The Misers," by Quentin Matsys. There were the two old gentlemen, with rich jewels in their caps—which, by the way, modern misers dispense with—counting their *rouleaux* of gold. There were the deeds and parchments, the scales for weighing the gold, the strong-boxes, and the parrot. But what modern miser would keep a parrot? Snatchit, as he looked at it, thought that it was a fanciful addition by the painter, and perhaps he was right. This picture, which interested old Sep very much, was so bright in its colours, its gold so glittering, its rich velvets so glowing, that it looked like a transparency.

The two misers, especially he who leans upon the shoulder of the other, seemed quite alive, and winked and grinned at their brother on the bed; so that there seemed to be a confidence established between the figure and the man.

"Ah, ha!" thought he, "those misers were wise men. They were no addle-pated fellows, who troubled themselves about politics, parliament, speakers, orators, or poets, and all such stuff. They would not let the good things escape them. How cunningly that one weighs the gold! Wise men! wise men! they looked after the main chance!"

As he said this, the picture brightened up wonderfully, and then faded down as suddenly, leaving in its stead a blank semi-translucent space, upon which another figure began to grow. This figure was not so much to Mr. Snatchit's taste. In the picture one miser had vanished, and in his place sat a grim, ghastly, grisly Death,—a skeleton, of course,—a bony, angular, bare, intruding fellow; a chap-fallen, mean rascal; a pusher into other men's places. There he sat, wearing another man's gown and cap, and grinning (as of course he does—he cannot shut his mouth, and shows all his teeth) at his partner weighing gold. Over his shoulder he carried a palmer's staff, and on the staff hung a small bottle, upon which was written, in small jets of a glow-worm brightness, "Thou fool! this night shalt thy soul be required!" One bony finger pointed to the legend; but the remaining miser took no heed of it, and went on calmly weighing and testing each single piece as before.

We have said that the picture was not so much to old Sep's taste as the former. In fact, he declared it to be a vile caricature, and would have given anything—so he said—to punish the artist.

"What's the man doing," he cried, "that that fellow, that thin, dirty jobbernowl there, should sit and grin at him? Looking after his gold, is he not? And do you call that wicked?"

The Death in the picture seemed to nod his head.

"Oh, you do, do you? you fool! you ass! you thick, brainless numbskull! Why, is he not doing what all the world considers right? The police won't interfere, will they?—eh, stupid? Does he not provide for his family? Does he not get troops of friends by it? Is it not a beautiful, bright, glistening object? Is it not clean—oh, so clean and nice! it does not dirty anyone's fingers to handle—does it, stupid—eh?"

The old wide mouth shook his head again.

"A fool!" continued Sep, with increasing warmth; "a sweet, light, goodly lustre it hath; it is more worth looking at than the sun! Sweet it is to get, sweet to hold! It makes labour light, a long day short, a grim brow a merry one! It buys friends, relations, love,—lots of it—lots, lots t—its mere name and reputation will do that! It quickens the brain, makes the dull man clever, the purblind sharp-sighted, the silly man a judge, the weak- brained fellow wise! Your next-door neighbour, hearing you have it, will desire to know you! The ladies will follow you, offering you the spoils of Sisera, rich garments, slaves and virgins, chariots and horses, places, parks, fair views, good reputation, name, place, power, wisdom, everything but—"

The bareboned fellow only answered this by extending his bony finger, and touching the miser in the picture, who gave one painful sigh, and one long, disturbed, uneasy stare, as if he could not comprehend the message, and fell back as the light and picture faded out.

This practical kind of answer Sep considered very rude, and turned away in a huff to look round the room at the effect which his breath had had elsewhere. Everywhere it was magical. The room was furnished, not only with viands and rich wines, but with guests. He had blown a beautiful carpet on the floor, a splendid rug, and a very fine fender before the fire. He blew sconces with candles—silver sconces and wax candles—against the walls. He blew holly up behind the pictures; the dressing-glass into a splendid mirror; the soap into a beautiful dish of trifle; the ewer into a silver claret-jug; and the basin into—what do you think?—why, into a large bowl of snap-dragon!

Such a party, such a feast, such snap-dragon! All the people who hated him—and they were many—were there; and in the flaming bowl were all the deeds, bonds, leases, wills, and mortgages he held in his possession, together with all the bags of money in the bank. Merrily danced the flame with a lurid light. As old Septimus grasped the bowl, sitting up in his bed, his guests pressed around him, and began to play. One snatched a will—that was a parson; another a lease—that was a lawyer; a third a bond—that was a farmer; and then each, with moping and mowing lips, blew out the blue flames, and carried away their prey.

Old Septimus grasped the bowl in terrible fright; and, in his eagerness to keep all, stretched his thin hands over the burning flame, only getting them singed; whilst his agile guests, one by one, picked out what they wanted, till all was gone; and then the flame died down to nothing, and the empty bowl was left in the miser's hands. Oh! what a shriek he gave; but none came to help him. His tormenting guests then blew out the splendid lights, pocketed the silver spoons and candlesticks, ran away with the claret-jug, and trooped out of the house with triumphant shouts of laughter. Those shouts broke the old man's heart. With a shriek of despair he fell back upon his bed, dead!—stone dead!

★★★★★★

"I am ready to contend," said the physician. Doctor Quartus, who was a great man in the eyes of the country apothecary, "that had my unfortunate brother obeyed his better nature, and joined with us at our Christmas party, he would have been here today. He died from mere inanition. People want shaking up sometimes."

"They do indeed," cried Mr. Cocks, the apothecary, suiting the action to the word with a black draught he held in his hand; "I am happy to find that so, experienced a practitioner agrees with me. If the departed gentleman had roused himself like."

"And had forgotten business, and visited the poor on Christmas-eve, and had come to church with us in the morning."

"To look at the red holly, and the red cheeks of the pretty children," said the soldier Tertius.

"And to have heard the hymn," interposed Quartus, who was fond of music.

"And to have eaten a good dinner," added Sextus, from the city.

"All these things have their use," said the physician, "especially physically."

"And morally too," answered the clergyman. "Poor fellow! poor Septimus! he lived alone, and died alone. His wealth will be divided amongst us, for he has left no will."

"It was all because he refused to come and play at snap-dragon," said the physician. "Enjoyment is not so useless as he thought it. It is good to be merry sometimes, even if it be only once a year."

So that was the verdict of the doctor—sudden deaths because he would not play at snap-dragon. Ah! it is all very well; but the doctor did not know what a dreadful game old Septimus *had* played. Ah! the public does. Let the public keep the secret.

Story Told in a Dream

Kubla Khan, some of the most exquisite verse ever penned, was dreamt by Coleridge, and written down afterwards, until interrupted by a stranger, whereby Coleridge and the public lost the continuation. This story also can claim affinity to ghosts and phantoms, simply by being dreamt— every word of it, by the author—some two or three years ago, and afterwards put in MS.

Told in a Dream

Some time before the first revolution of France, when the whole surface of that great kingdom was agitated, as a brow is wrinkled by deep and serious thought, there lived in Paris an honest workman named Pierre Laroche. He was a gunsmith, and worked laboriously at his vocation; not wasting his time in *fêtes*, dancings, and junketings, but spending his quiet evenings with his book, looking on the great events passing around him, and endeavouring to raise himself in intellect, in usefulness, and in worth. Those, therefore, of his fellow-workmen who were light and giddy of disposition, sneered and laughed, and called him "sullen Pierre;" but he accounted for his stolid manner by saying that he had some of the burgher blood of English Calais in him, as indeed he had, his mother coming from that town.

Now it chanced that Laroche, in going daily to his work, met, and almost always at the self-same spot, a pretty and neatly-dressed young woman, who passed on to her daily labour also, being a flower-maker.

Elise d'Orville—for that was her name—was as pretty an object as you could wish to bless your sight. Tall, gracefully formed, with fair complexion, and blue, laughing eyes, it was not to be marvelled that Master Pierre looked forward every mom to see her, and sometimes, too, for many, many mornings, looking beyond the present time, wondering if she would be his wife or not.

Nor is it very surprising that her cheek mantled and her eyes fell as they met his deep and earnest gaze, and that then, half ashamed, she would raise them with a sunny laugh, and so pass on; so that, even before they well knew, they loved each other, and looked with all the quicksightedness of affection to each other. Yet neither had courage to testify more; and so passed time away, till fortune did that for them which brought them nearer to each other; which was thus: one morning Elise stumbled, and would have fallen, had not Pierre happened to have run forward and helped her.

And hereon their acquaintance ripened each day, till Pierre thought it full time to declare his love; so the next morning, being early to his business, and she also, led, possibly, by that instinct which guides all lovers, Pierre, turning back, went with her, and by the way declared his love in such earnest tones as she could not mistake; but, frightened at his earnestness, she told him that she loved him as a sister, and not yet firmly enough to become his wife.

"Oh, Elise!" said he, holding both her hands in his, "a sister's love, with all its intensity, its unselfishness, and its devotion, will scarce suffice me in a wife. You must love me more, or else we here part; for even as I give my heart to you, so I expect in return yours totally, solely."

Then she laughingly replied,—"Why, what a tyrant art thou!—you would scarce have me forget my maiden modesty and become a wooer to thee, Pierre? I love thee"—and here her voice faltered slightly—"more than ever yet I loved man or woman."

He was soothed at this; and thinking, more in answer to her look than words, that if she did not now love him, love would grow with years, knowing what deep love he had in his own heart, caressed her gently, and soon after took her for his wife.

Some time passed happily enough, and a little son was born, on whom Pierre doted; but shortly after this his wife's gay spirits became clouded, and she longed for merrier company and richer clothes than Pierre could well afford. Besides this, his inclinations were different to hers, and his home studious and quiet. Neighbours, too, spake to the pretty Elise, and told her of gay *fêtes* and dances, and how merrily and wildly the world went on around them, whilst they but droned at home. Pierre, as you may suppose, quicksighted, as all people of deep affections are, soon saw the change, and groaned in great anguish over it. He did what he could, too, to remove it, and to renovate his wife's affections, but in vain. Alas! Elise, light and giddy, saw with different eyes than heretofore.

Now at this juncture it chanced that a cousin of his wife's, a man of high station and well born (for some had said Elise had married beneath her station), meeting her at a mutual friend's house, renewed his acquaintance, and frequently visited her at her home. He was a courtier, of handsome exterior, and possessing dangerous talents, which he knew well how to use. His morality was that of the court of Louis XV., and to this he added an insinuating and polished address, a gentle manner, and an engaging wit. Pierre noticed his frequent visits to his wife, and her increasing coldness; but he scarce knew what to do; and so, waiting in misery for some higher prompting, his fate broke upon him at once.

He returned home one night, and as he approached the door saw no light; he felt a sense of loneliness and desolation, and as he lifted the latch of the little cottage, he heard the low sobs of his child. Smitten with a sudden fear, he dared not call his wife— he dreaded the silence which would ensue; he called to his child, and asked him where his mother was. The boy knew not: she had wept over him ere he went to bed, and he had awakened in the evening and found himself alone. Pierre, doubting his ears, struck a light and looked round the room. On his wife's dressing-table, which he had taken so much care to adorn, he found a letter bearing his name: he tore it open, and it ran thus:—

Pierre Laroche,—
I have removed my cousin from thy roof to a more suit-able, sphere—a place where she will be more appreciated than in thy dull home. Thou wilt find inclosed a draft for an amount sufficient for thee, but inadequate for the jewel I have taken from you. Thine,

Denis Rochaigne.

The room swam round Laroche as he stared wildly again at the letter, and then fell down on the floor as if dead. His little boy was shivering and crying over him when he recovered. He rose to his knees and prayed, and then comforted his child. In the morning you could scarcely see any trace of his deep grief, with the exception of his calmness and sunken eyes. He spoke not to the neighbours who crowded to him, and in a few days had removed from his old home to a distant part of Paris.

Night after night now found Pierre seeking in the grand quarters of the town the dwelling of his enemy, the Count Ro-chaigne. For months he was unsuccessful; the guilty pair had fled to Italy at first, and it was long ere Laroche found any clue to them. At length he was successful. The next night saw him armed with pistols and rapier, and dressed in a dark suit closely fitting his tall form. He was shortly at the hotel of Rochaigne, a large building standing on the outskirts of the town. He en-tered, passing the porter on the stairs, who thought him one of the guests, for Rochaigne was gay, entertaining his companions; wine and delicate meats were spread before them: he started as Laroche entered, and turned colour, shouting,—

"What want you, fellow?"

"Mine honour," said the gunsmith, quietly, "or satisfaction."

"Ha, ha!" laughed the aristocrat, "we give not satisfaction to such as you. You had money."

"Money!" shouted Pierre, "'tis there;" and he flung the crum-pled paper in Rochaigne's face. "Take this,"—and he held forth a pistol.

"'Tis well made enough," said the count, taking it; "if you want to sell it, here's money. As for your wife, you may take her back: at least, you might, had not a friend, of mine begged her of me."

With a howl of rage Laroche flung down the other pistol and drew his sword; but the surprised guests were before him, and rushing on him, disarmed him and thrust him down stairs. His object was thwarted and crushed, and years passed before the gunsmith met Rochaigne again.

★★★★★★

Years had passed, we said: the face of France had changed: a great golf had opened between the people and the nobles, and blood had run like water. Pierre Laroche had made himself a name. Eloquent he was of speech; his words came like a torrent on his hearers' hearts. Whatever wrong they suffered, whatever feudal oppression, which for years had grown up like a giant fungus on their liberty, he expounded and set forth. Fearless, untiring, of wondrous research and learning, he was a dangerous enemy to the class which he opposed. Crowds flocked to him, and he became a recognized leader, not only by words but by example. His son also, grown up by this time to a tall stripling of sixteen, inherited his father's hatred for the aristocracy, and worked and helped him.

His mother, the unfortunate Elise, so dearly loved and yet so slight of love herself, had perished miserably. Her unclaimed body lay for some time at the Morgue, till someone unknown buried the suicide. And Rochaigne, the libertine, where is he? Prosperous—to all appearance happy, a colonel, too, of cuirassiers, and the sunlight that glances from his breastplate is not more bright than the silky smile which plays upon his face. He is now at the head of his regiment; *they* are faithful to the king, at least as yet, and go to dislodge some rioters who have made themselves troublesome.

"*Peste!*" swears the colonel, "the *canaille* are stiff fighters; why, their very women fight like devils. But forward, we will trample them to dust."

Pierre Laroche and a few of his men, true citizens of Paris, were behind a small heap of pavement hastily thrown up. They saw the *cuirassiers* approach; a slight tremor came upon them, like a ruffling of water by the wind, and then the teeth were firmlier set, the hand more tightly clenched, and the stock of the musket fitted more closely to the shoulder.

"They come, boys," whispered Pierre;—"there are two deaths, one glorious, one shameful; choose,—they are upon us."

A look of confidence, cheerily given, answered him, and for one moment his eye softened as he turned to his young son, who, with a boy's enthusiasm, sat calmly by his side, elated at the prospect of the coming struggle; but he muttered one word,—it was "Elise," and then glared through the rude loophole upon the soldiers.

"Now!" cried Pierre; and then from every crack or ragged hole, from window and from door, blazed forth a shower of bullets. The soldiers reeled and broke, and then gave way and fell back to the rear; but Rochaigne, with fresh men, rode up and brought them off, at the same time encouraging his men with voice and gesture.

"Again, boys! again!" he cried; "what will the fair dames of France say to us, conquered by a few of the scourings of the Faubourg St. Antoine? Now for a gallant charge."

A hundred spurs were stricken rowel-deep, and a loud shout of defiance rose, as with a spring and a bound they reached the barricade; but shout answered shout, and the deadly shower blazed forth as before; the men sprang across the barriers, too, and fought with the dismounted cavalry. Rochaigne's horse had fallen, and his helmet, unloosened in the fray, rolled off.

"Father," cried the boy, struck with the face, which had frowned on his infancy, and knowing the story of his father's wrongs, "'tis he—Rochaigne!"

"Where, boy, where?" shouted the gunsmith.

"Here," cried the boy, bounding over the barrier and striking at the colonel.

The officer, with a contemptuous smile, caught the lad in his strong grasp and raised his sword. Pierre's gun was at his shoulder, and his eyes swam; suddenly there grew before his mind the whole of his life, and by its side the contrast what it *might* have been had not Rochaigne cursed him with his presence. He pulled the trigger—there was a sharp report and a crash—he waved away the smoke with his hand, and looked forth, and saw his son's eyes shine with unearthly brightness, and in his forehead a small round hole, whence the blood gushed forth as the boy fell prone. Rochaigne's arm was arrested by his wonder, and the next moment, in a lull of the battle, he heard the shriek with which the brave gunsmith broke his heart as he fell dead behind the barrier.

The Laying of the Ghosts

Childish fancies, mists of error,
Witch, and gnome, and elfin sprite.
Ye no longer create terror;
Quick begone and vanish quite.
Leave us to our modern knowledge.
To the wisdom Science boasts;
'Tis long since that school and college
Far have banished faith in "Ghosts."

Tricksy Puck and winsome Fairy—
Creatures of the poet's brain,—
Ye have left your dwellings airy,—
Darkling wood, lone heath, or plain.
Not one lass will entertain ye,
Not a shepherd play your host;
Yet I question here, what gain we?
Since we welcome grimmer ghosts.

Ghosts of Folly, ghosts of Passion,
Withered sprites of Hate and Pride,
In the awful, ancient fashion.
Through brain-chambers mope and glide.
Ghosts of Avarice, Ambition,
Yet troop out o'er England's coasts:
Let us own, with sad contrition,
We are haunted still by ghosts.

Error ever crowned Immortal;

Lisping Folly lives and sings;
Elves are chased from our portal,
Whilst we welcome meaner things.
Jaundiced Money, the calf golden.
Counts his worshippers by hosts;
Oh! far better was the olden
Honesty and faith in ghosts.

Times are changing, seasons fading;
Let us onwards through the fair;
Hasten to lay down the lading
We have gathered here and there.
Feuds long past we yet remember.
Wrongs unredressed we cherish most;
Greed and Hate—stamp out each ember.
'Tis brave laying such grim ghosts.

Welcome next the kindlier spirits.
Gentle Love and Faith in kind.
Which the human heart inherits.
If out of sight and out of mind.
Like St. Patrick, chase the vermin;
He shall be rewarded most—
Not with coronet and ermine—
When we all—give up the ghost.

LEONAUR

ALSO FROM LEONAUR
AVAILABLE IN SOFTCOVER OR HARDCOVER WITH DUST JACKET

THE COLLECTED SUPERNATURAL AND WEIRD FICTION OF J. SHERIDAN LE FANU: VOLUME 1 *by J. Sheridan le Fanu*—Contains Two Novels 'The Haunted Baronet' and 'The Evil Guest', One Novella 'Carmilla',One Novelette and Ten Short Stories of the Ghostly and Gothic.

THE COLLECTED SUPERNATURAL AND WEIRD FICTION OF J. SHERIDAN LE FANU: VOLUME 2 *by J. Sheridan le Fanu*—Contains One Novel 'Uncle Silas', One Novelette 'Green Tea' and Five Short Stories of the Ghostly and Gothic.

THE COLLECTED SUPERNATURAL AND WEIRD FICTION OF J. SHERIDAN LE FANU: VOLUME 3 *by J. Sheridan le Fanu*—Contains One Novel 'The House by the Churchyard', and One Short Story 'Dickon the Devil' of the Ghostly and Gothic.

THE COLLECTED SUPERNATURAL AND WEIRD FICTION OF J. SHERIDAN LE FANU: VOLUME 4 *by J. Sheridan le Fanu*—Contains One Novel 'The Wyvern Mystery', One Novelette 'Mr. Justice Harbottle,' and Nine Short Stories of the Ghostly and Gothic.

THE COLLECTED SUPERNATURAL AND WEIRD FICTION OF J. SHERIDAN LE FANU: VOLUME 5 *by J. Sheridan le Fanu*—Contains One Novel 'The Rose and the Key', One Novelette 'Spalatro, From the Notes of Fra Giacomo', and Two Short Stories of the Ghostly and Gothic

THE COLLECTED SUPERNATURAL AND WEIRD FICTION OF J. SHERIDAN LE FANU: VOLUME 6 *by J. Sheridan le Fanu*—Contains One Novel 'Checkmate', and Six Short Stories of the Ghostly and Gothic

THE COLLECTED SUPERNATURAL AND WEIRD FICTION OF J. SHERIDAN LE FANU: VOLUME 7 *by J. Sheridan le Fanu*—Contains Two Novels 'All in the Dark' and 'The Room in the Dragon Volant', Two Novelettes 'The Mysterious Lodger' and 'The Watcher' and Four Short Stories of the Ghostly and Gothic

THE COLLECTED SUPERNATURAL AND WEIRD FICTION OF J. SHERIDAN LE FANU: VOLUME 8 *by J. Sheridan le Fanu*—Contains One Novel 'A Lost Name', One Novelette 'The Last Heir of Castle Connor', and Six Short Stoies of the Ghostly and Gothic

ALSO FROM LEONAUR
AVAILABLE IN SOFTCOVER OR HARDCOVER WITH DUST JACKET

THE COMPLETE FOUR JUST MEN: VOLUME 2 *by Edgar Wallace—The Law of the Four Just Men & The Three Just Men*—disillusioned with a world where the wicked and the abusers of power perpetually go unpunished, the Just Men set about to rectify matters according to their own standards, and retribution is dispensed on swift and deadly wings.

THE COMPLETE RAFFLES: 1 *by E. W. Hornung—The Amateur Cracksman & The Black Mask*—By turns urbane gentleman about town and accomplished cricketer, life is just too ordinary for Raffles and that sets him on a series of adventures that have long been treasured as a real antidote to the 'white knights' who are the usual heroes of the crime fiction of this period.

THE COMPLETE RAFFLES: 2 *by E. W. Hornung—A Thief in the Night & Mr Justice Raffles*—By turns urbane gentleman about town and accomplished cricketer, life is just too ordinary for Raffles and that sets him on a series of adventures that have long been treasured as a real antidote to the 'white knights' who are the usual heroes of the crime fiction of this period.

THE COLLECTED SUPERNATURAL AND WEIRD FICTION OF WILKIE COLLINS: VOLUME 1 *by Wilkie Collins*—Contains one novel 'The Haunted Hotel', one novella 'Mad Monkton', three novelettes 'Mr Percy and the Prophet', 'The Biter Bit' and 'The Dead Alive' and eight short stories to chill the blood.

THE COLLECTED SUPERNATURAL AND WEIRD FICTION OF WILKIE COLLINS: VOLUME 2 *by Wilkie Collins*—Contains one novel 'The Two Destinies', three novellas 'The Frozen deep', 'Sister Rose' and 'The Yellow Mask' and two short stories to chill the blood.

THE COLLECTED SUPERNATURAL AND WEIRD FICTION OF WILKIE COLLINS: VOLUME 3 *by Wilkie Collins*—Contains one novel 'Dead Secret,' two novelettes 'Mrs Zant and the Ghost' and 'The Nun's Story of Gabriel's Marriage' and five short stories to chill the blood.

FUNNY BONES *selected by Dorothy Scarborough*—An Anthology of Humorous Ghost Stories.

MONTEZUMA'S CASTLE AND OTHER WEIRD TALES *by Charles B. Cory*—Cory has written a superb collection of eighteen ghostly and weird stories to chill and thrill the avid enthusiast of supernatural fiction.

SUPERNATURAL BUCHAN *by John Buchan*—Stories of Ancient Spirits, Uncanny Places & Strange Creatures.

LEONAUR

ALSO FROM LEONAUR
AVAILABLE IN SOFTCOVER OR HARDCOVER WITH DUST JACKET

MR MUKERJI'S GHOSTS *by S. Mukerji*—Supernatural tales from the British Raj period by India's Ghost story collector.

KIPLINGS GHOSTS *by Rudyard Kipling*—Twelve stories of Ghosts, Hauntings, Curses, Werewolves & Magic.

THE COLLECTED SUPERNATURAL AND WEIRD FICTION OF WASHINGTON IRVING: VOLUME 1 *by Washington Irving*—Including one novel 'A History of New York', and nine short stories of the Strange and Unusual.

THE COLLECTED SUPERNATURAL AND WEIRD FICTION OF WASHINGTON IRVING: VOLUME 2 *by Washington Irving*—Including three novelettes 'The Legend of the Sleepy Hollow', 'Dolph Heyliger', 'The Adventure of the Black Fisherman' and thirty-two short stories of the Strange and Unusual.

THE COLLECTED SUPERNATURAL AND WEIRD FICTION OF JOHN KENDRICK BANGS: VOLUME 1 *by John Kendrick Bangs*—Including one novel 'Toppleton's Client or A Spirit in Exile', and ten short stories of the Strange and Unusual.

THE COLLECTED SUPERNATURAL AND WEIRD FICTION OF JOHN KENDRICK BANGS: VOLUME 2 *by John Kendrick Bangs*—Including four novellas 'A House-Boat on the Styx', 'The Pursuit of the House-Boat', 'The Enchanted Typewriter' and 'Mr. Munchausen' of the Strange and Unusual.

THE COLLECTED SUPERNATURAL AND WEIRD FICTION OF JOHN KENDRICK BANGS: VOLUME 3 *by John Kendrick Bangs*—Including twor novellas 'Olympian Nights', 'Roger Camerden: A Strange Story', and ten short stories of the Strange and Unusual.

THE COLLECTED SUPERNATURAL AND WEIRD FICTION OF MARY SHELLEY: VOLUME 1 *by Mary Shelley*—Including one novel 'Frankenstein or the Modern Prometheus', and fourteen short stories of the Strange and Unusual.

THE COLLECTED SUPERNATURAL AND WEIRD FICTION OF MARY SHELLEY: VOLUME 2 *by Mary Shelley*—Including one novel 'The Last Man', and three short stories of the Strange and Unusual.

THE COLLECTED SUPERNATURAL AND WEIRD FICTION OF AMELIA B. EDWARDS *by Amelia B. Edwards*—Contains two novelettes 'Monsieur Maurice', and 'The Discovery of the Treasure Isles', one ballad 'A Legend of Boisguilbert' and seventeen short stories to cill the blood.

www.ingramcontent.com/pod-product-compliance
Lightning Source LLC
Chambersburg PA
CBHW030508260626
47157CB00005B/1699